Your Place Or Will It Be My Place

Ana's Early Life Comes Around In The Form Of A Dragon Female

Donna is looking at this younger woman and trying to figure out why in the hell she cannot get the message she is not interested in her at all. She lets her inside. Her first mistake she knew it the moment she opens her door. She was pinning her up on her double wide refrigerator. Kissed her firmly as she holds her arms over her head. Please stop Terry. I want you Donna. She trying to knee her in her crotch. She was taller than Donna she fights to get her arms down. She made it. Only because her Teddy Bear was nipping her ankles. Terry was trying to get him to stop. But he was not afraid of this woman.

His human was being attacked. From her tone of voice knew she was upset, and he can tell she was afraid. She was moving slowly as Terry was still trying to get her to give in. She makes it to the door. Grabs the handle finds the lock unlocks it. She tells her brave boy. Get Mira. Hurry boy. Terry shuts the door. Quickly. Mira saw her girlfriend's dog running fast to her. Barking. She tells him I will go help her. You go to Sandy. He was barking at Sandy's. Sandy knew it was Teddy Bear. It was clear Donna was being attacked by someone. She grabs a lethal injection. She always has one or two ready, to use when it was an emergency. She can feel the tension from Mira.

Ana pulls beside Sandy where are you heading. To Donna's. Unlock the door. She does. They see Teddy Bear running back to his mama. She was saying to Terry. You cannot have me. I will not let you take me from my Mira. She cannot have you. That was too much. Mira forced the door open. Has a Billy club. She has just enough room she whispers deck down now my love. She did. Terry was hit hard. She clasped in front of Donna. Donna was lifted. Be careful Mira. Teddy Bear is behind you. Move Teddy Bear. He hears his mama talking to him. You are a good boy. He knows the other two well. Ana had sent a message to the paranormal police. They were dragging the dazed Terry out of Donna's travel trailer. Mira was not letting her out of her sight. Come boy. Ana has his leash. Mira saw the Red Lady Ops were at work fixing the door with paranormal police watching her place. The nosy neighbors were trying to find out what was going on. But it was already over.

Mira was kissing her Donna. Sandy was saying. Mira, please let me check her over. She finally does when she saw her birth mama looking at her. Powder Puff had been the one to help her mama from her sleeping place. She felt her oldest girl, girlfriend was in danger. She was on the plane with her child Power Puff. She was flying her mama directly to the town. Anna was there to rush her to Mira's. She was beside her. Donna are you okay baby? Hi. Who are you. Sorry. I am Mira's and Powder Puff's mama. Their birth mama. Flame comes to see her daughter-in-law. How are you Donna. She risked being seen in her dragon. Who are you? I am Mira's and Powder Puff's alpha mama. I am Flame. It was not lost on them even Catharina. That her mate used her true name. I am Catharina my child. I felt you were in danger from my oldest feelings. They both had. Donna was smiling at all of them.

Anna was looking at her too. She goes to get a blanket to cover her tempting body from view. Thank you, Anna. Anna just smiles. She leaves to see how things were going at her place. Caught the weasel neighbor trying to peek into her place. When she lifted him up, she throws him to the God. Nice catch male. Ben was away on another matter. He older mate was there. He had noticed his alpha mama had flown into his large yard. He left her something to wear as she changed into her human. Thank you, my big baby boy. She kissed his check. I am going to Mira's.

She saw that many of the Goddesses were there blocking any lookie lou's getting too close. Donna was too important to the family. She holds a secret not many knew. She first told her girlfriend Mira. Mira told her family. Mira was the one to be allowed to be her mate. She was hiding in her human. She was even more important than Anna. Anna knew it. But they will not tell anyone all her history. Ana went to her secret child she had been the alpha mama to a beautiful dragon baby. She was visiting her without an older female to watch she was not to have the older lover she was given to show her how she would give herself to a female. Ana had taken her, and they knew she was pregnant with Ana's young. The female was sent away. Mina had not known why Ana was watched so much when she was younger. But soon her disgrace with the older dragon was forgiven. Mira happened to be lucky she was the one she gave her heart too. With Catharina and Flame now there, Donna will have the protection she will need.

Anna was surprised she has an older sister still living. She felt protective of her big sister. Later when she could she was talking to her birth mama. They talked about the older dragon female. Baby she was only to teach me about the importance of being a good mate. She had taught me so much. I guess I got carried away and I was found out that I was the one to make her pregnant as young as I was. I was watched for a long time. I was always kept close to home.

Mina happened to move to our pack with her own mamas. The history of my own family goes back to the first female that found her attraction to another female. It was a law set by males no female will be allowed to mate with another female. My great, great grand dame and her lover did. And ran a long time to be with the females from the two packs. So, the males would not find them. Anna was listening and lets her mama talk about their family. She always did love hearing it. They learned they were both seers. Another taboo males had order was not going to allow females to do. I became a seer incredibly early. It grew over the years.

Seeing your sister brings back so much. She carries the birth mark you and I have baby. Grinning the large clit too. Anna said I saw it mama. I had to cover her tempting body. Thank you, for that child. She tells her she has the extra-long tits too. Anna was smiling. I was told my own had to be cut. But I had Sandy conceal it instead when I went up to the clouds. I had it corrected thanks to Sandy. Just after your sister came to move here. Mina was at the door. She was looking at her ex-mate.

Come inside Mina. She was not looking happy with Ana. She gets right to the point. When were you going to tell me about my stepchild Ana. Sandy was let inside. Calm down Mina. Mina I was ordered to not tell you or anyone. I was 16. Donna's mama was my teacher in how to enjoy having my body taken by another female. She was blamed of course. But I wanted to show her how much I had learned from her. I was surprised I could make her pregnant. But we all could. We no longer needed a male. Mina smiles at her oldest. Moves the hair that seems to always get in her eyes. Anna just smiles. Ana may I be part of Donna's life too. Ana gets up from her chair goes to hug her. Then steps back. Thank you, Mina. I see no reason why not.

They hear wings then a tall female knocking on Ana's and Rocky's place. The female moves when a female pulls into the driveway. Rocky blocks her from her home. Ana comes out to her mate. Noticed the beautiful dragon. She was dress. Ana my dear. You have grown into a grand lady. She sees Anna. Hello my dear. And high Goddess. You are much like your beautiful mama. Mina I assume. Yes, I am. Alpha mama to this beautiful female. Yes, I am. She is looking at Rocky. You are the mate to Ana. Standing straighter. I have been 450 years female. How wonderful. May I speak to you then. Ana was told she will be right back. Rocky was surprised by her request. As the first mate I wish to request to be part of their arrangement to be theirs together as second mate. Told her to think about it and talk to her Ana. She asked where her child was. Rocky told her. She walks to her child's mate's motorhome. She was greeted by her child's mama-in-laws. Catharina! Karan! You look wonderful female. My first mate Flame. Hello. You must be Donna's birth mama. Yes, I am. Is she available to see me? Donna was in her birth mama's strong arms. Mira came out. You are the oldest of two. Yes, I am. First born. My twin brother lives here too. You are a powerful female. So is your beautiful child. I wished to let you know I have asked Rocky to see if Ana will allow me to be their shared second mate. Oh, mama how wonderful. Catharina has mixed feelings for Karan. Ana would want to have her perhaps.

As they were talking at Mira's. Ana was thinking how she can handle having two so alike. She looks at her loyal Rocky. Waiting for her thoughts on this. She finally came to Ana. Ana I will always be yours right. Yes, my Rocky. We have been together 450 years. I am wanting what makes us happy. Okay. Calling over the Mira's. Please ask Karan to return to our place. Yes Rocky. You are being asked to return to their place. She runs to their place. Smacks a male trying to take her. He was dead from that smack. Ben saw a female rushing to Ana's he calls the crime clean up unit. They were already coming. They had waited for the male to do something stupid. She was inside being held by both. She was shaken she had just killed in plain sight of a male. Ana tells her. He works for my big baby mate. She looks at both. Rocky said mate too. She was smiling. Thank you both. I had only had Ana and for a short time to know I was not wanting Catharina. I would not allow another female to touch me. She looks at Ana. Ana sees a look she was reacting to. Then turned her attention fully on Rocky. She watched as both help her undress. She watched as they were undressing. They ran to the king size bed. With Karan in the middle. They both knew she was desperately needing their loving. She was not young. They told her they wanted to make her a Goddesses. She will be with them a lot longer. Life mate is what they were offering her.

They lead her to their bed. She was given a workout she has really needed. She looks at both. You two sure have a lot more skills than I do. I was with Catharina for a short time after I had been with you 5 hundred years before. I happen to see her coming from her place she sleeps. It did not work in my opinion. She might think different. I knew where I wanted to be. Thank you Rocky for allowing me to have the joy to be mated to you both. My pleasure female. Catharina might want to ask if they can join us. I hope you both will say no. Ana makes a call to Catharina. Hello Ana. My dear. We have claimed Karan as our shared second mate. She had asked Rocky to think on it. Rocky was the one she asked first.

Catharina seem to be disappointed. Okay Ana. Thank you for telling me. She had told me so long ago she did not feel we were compatible for each other. She is right of course. Flame wants me to say yes. We do work good together. From the looks of our young. Night Ana. Night Catharina. Catharina wanted young from the beautiful dragon. At the time she was still feeling the shame of what had happen. But seeing their baby all grownup and mated to the oldest of Catharina. How odd it had happened that way. Karan was showing she was having Ana's young. Rocky had been working her long shift. She was also pregnant by Ana. When she saw the young, they had she was glad she made the right choice. Ana was pregnant with her Rocky's young. As it should be. She was simply happy to be back in the life of her now Goddess mate and her second Goddess mate. When she wanted to fly in her full dragon, she was surprised to learn Ana and Rocky were also dragons.

Having her two mates flying with her felt wonderful. She was surprised when they were returning to Dublin, Ireland. She sees as they glide down to their Castle. She watched as they remove something. She follows them inside the underground nest. There was plenty of nesting to make their nest. She was smiling to know she has with the right females. They hear large wings landing on the outside. Saw a female checking out the place for her own use. Not knowing the owners were not pleased. She sees 3 females coming after her. She flies off to find another nesting place. She was finding the next pair were respective to her. She was taken as their second mate. She was in heat.

Bumba watched how her mate handled her new shared mate. They were all pregnant. Ginny was a virgin too. Accepting her new life with her first mates ever. She was not she tells her alpha mate going to return to her mamas, castle now. She was to mate a female she has never wanted as her mate. It was to be a big party that day. Anna tells her mama she has the female that she warned off. She was now her shared mate with Bumba. She was trying to hide from her own mamas trying to have her mate a female she does not want. Okay baby. I took her virgin body as my mate. Bumba has been with her. She will be safer. Yes baby. We will of course help protect her. Thank you, mama.

The females had moved into Anna's and her mama's land. They would soon learn an older dragon that was as powerful would drive them from their territory. 4 were Goddesses. As they follow the scent of their oldest that was in heat. But as they get closer. They smell the true owners coming directly as the much larger dragons. They can tell they are the Goddesses. Their oldest has been claimed by the High Goddess and her first mate. Even Bumba is well known as her loyal mate. Their bond was strong. Then they smell her birth mama. They were finding of a sudden more Goddesses. One is another stronger Goddess. She is well known as well. The oldest know Goddess was there.

The females were forced to go from Ireland. Told to not go near American. She owns several territories out there. The female who was to be given to the oldest had made it seem she was the rightful owner of the territory where the scent of the true owner was stronger. She was handled by Catharina. As the Ancient Goddess she can demand her death. Which she felt was right. The female was given what she deserved. She had forced her way into a royal dragon family then tried to take control of them. Even demanding their oldest. When they learned she had left her safe home to find a new place to call hers.

Found she was taken by the High Goddess. With her birth mama as her back up. The female who wanted the female that was protected and taken as the shared second to the High Goddess and her Loyal mate. Was now back in the role she was to be. A royal dragon. Anna handled the female so quickly she was shocked how she was handled. Her own mama came looking for that child who just could not be kept in her own family. The female was shocked to find her child had tried to take a female of royal blood as her mate.

She came to see Anna. But she waits in her human to be allowed to talk to the High Goddess. Ana went to the female. She stayed on her knees even as she was told she could stand. She has always been the lowest. Because of her shame to allow a female to take her before she was an adult. Ana lifts the female from her knees. She was told to look at her. She was taught, she has no right ever to look into the eyes of a grand female. But Ana lifts her chin. She closed her eyes. Ana hissed said, dam it female look into my eyes now. She does. Ana. Yes female. I am. You are the seer. Yes, I am. Who has taken your will to be yourself. The one who was the sister to your playmate Sarren. Where is she. I am here. She moves from the females. You get behind the last female now whore. She was going to do as she was ordered, but Ana said no. You go to the biggest female.

Ana said you will now answer for your own crime. Ana you are not the one who can order me around. Anna steps forward. Stands with her birth mama. Well look who is here. How are you sweet thing. Ana was not pleased when she directs her attention on her big baby. You will be respectful of whom you speak to. This female is even hotter than she had been as a child. Rocky was so quick. She slapped this rude female. You will never talk like that to the High Goddess or my mate the Second to the High Goddess. When she saw Mina with another female. She said, Mina you should tell your mate and pup to respect me. Mina said, the female who slapped you is her true mate. They have been mated 450 years. My child is no longer a pup. She is the High Goddess. The place she has earned. She has taken the pup who you dare to control. She is her mate. Bring that female to me now. She had not wanted your advances any more than I wanted them either. You are a cruel bitch. When she dares to walk up to Anna was going to touch her super-size breast. Was saying. I love to get you in my bed female. You are built so yummy. Anna has her on the ground. Bumba has been told to stay with our shared second. Go back inside my loyal mate. Rocky and Ana wanted in this fight. Rocky earned the right. When they walked away with her confined, she was not given the right to talk to them. They all see this High Goddess was a female who knew how to handle her now. When she was taken down so fast. The female has learned she has found a skilled fighter. She was not letting her get by with what she had as a young pup. But Ana had found her trying to take her baby as her plaything. She was crying by now.

Ana lets her mate handle her. Anna knows Rocky was always working out with her mama to be able to handle a female who dares to harm any female. She was a very protective female. She was doing it for both. Ana was getting hot to take her Rocky as soon as she can. Anna saw the love, lust and a lot more when she was watching her loyal mate. Rocky had surprised them when she broke her neck quickly. They watch her turn into her dragon. After she pulled her clothes off. Lifts the body. Anna and Ana were turning too. Following her to the ocean. They waited saw the dark shape coming fast. The female turned into her dragon after she had died.

Rocky drops her into the ocean watched as the megalodon begins to take large pieces of the dragon. When she was finished eating her full. Smaller sharks came for their share of the dragon meat. Soon the dragon was finished out. She lived an evil way of life. To end as shark dinner at the end. Taking what she felt was her right to take. To end up a meal for the creatures of the ocean deep once all over the ocean to a hand full only. Rocky has proven her skills to attack and kill when it called for it. Protecting females was all Goddesses roll to protect. Anna was so proud of Rocky. She was reinstated as 4th to the High Goddess. Rocky was finding her Ana was after her the moment they were back in their own Castle. Their shared mate watched the fun. She must learn how to make love to her mates. Watching them was a thrilling thing to see. They smell she has climaxed a lot watching their wild loving to each other. She was taken by both her mates. She was enjoying their attention. She was worn out after the workout she was given. She was curled up in the middle. They had turned into their werewolf for the night.

Anna was restless. Something was not feeling right. Ana woke her mates. Hurry girls they were looking around saw the smaller males coming. They did not know the owners of the land were watching them. They did not know this of course. That the females they had come for, were no longer there. When the females came from all around them, they learned their mistake. There were only 10 smaller males to over 200 females. They were finding they were still feeling the victory from the last encounter with a trespassing group of females. The battle ends quickly. Ben and his mates showed up after the battle was over. They were the ones to carry the male dragons to the ocean. Several megalodons were there waiting for this large meal. They came from all over. Smaller sharks waiting for their turn to feed as well. They will stay in Dublin, Ireland until their young are old enough to fly. There will be other battles to fight and protecting their young at the same time.

The Lady Who Sings To Jackie

Jackie is turning 68 today. She was living with her pets. She is lonely. You never know it when she came out greeting her neighbors. She helps some of the neighbors when she can. She has a heart to give to someone. But only men seem to want her. She does not want them. She wants a woman close to her age. Her one neighbor keeps telling her that if she going to sex. It will be a sin without being married. She has her own ideas about it of course. She keeps her life closed to her neighbor. She is a woman you keep from your own thoughts. And who you want in your bed or theirs.

At 68 she feels her life choices are her own business. What she writes is not her business either. She was writing awhile when she hears a woman singing by her window. She sees a beautiful woman smiling at her as she was still singing to her. Not losing a beat. She goes back Inside. Makes a tang cold drink for her. Takes it outside to her. She gives it to her. She drinks it down. Was going to give her, her own. She finished singing a beautiful song. She comes up to Jackie. Kissed her firmly. When she talks. She has a deep voice. Jackie was being held closely to her guest. You like to have your gift for your birthday. Trying to clear her head to be able to talk. All that came out was. Gift? Yes honey. I loved the song baby. She was grinning. She was backing her up opens the door. Still holding her. Lifts her up and goes into her crowded travel trailer. Shuts the door. Letting her down. But still holding to her body. She was moaning as she was kissed again. You are my dear as I had hoped for. Really? Yes dear.

The neighbor two spaces over came knocking. She steps away. She could see what she was needing. What is it, Nancy. Will you be able to help getting my laptop working. Hold a moment. She looks at the beautiful woman. She nods. I will be right there. She watched her leave. You come here she whispers. The woman does. You sure you want to stop this right now. I can go get things ready. You see where she went? Yes. Okay. Do not worry my dear. I can hold off giving you your birthday gift. She unzips her top placed her hands into her top. So, you know what I wish to give you, my mate. Jackie kissed her firmly. Has the slightly younger woman wanting her right now. I will be waiting in my motorhome. I must go to the office now. Breathless from Jackie's kiss. I will leave the number of my space under your rock big mama. She sees her get into a nice Peterbilt Rig. She shuts up her travel trailer.

Jackie walks to her neighbor's 5th wheel. Let's, her know she was there to work on her laptop. She gets it online goes to find her books and again saved the location so it could be reached. The woman keeps letting another neighbor help her. And it's not good. Because he always uses his own password making it so she would need to go to him instead. But she has it all done and corrected for her. Again, she blocks his attempts to use her account with Amazona. But Jackie believes in not doing what he does. The last laptop crashed. Jackie again protects the woman's accounts. Telling her once again to not allow him to do anything he can use his own passwords to get her information. He was slowly drawing enough attention to his crimes. Ordering things for his own use. She is so overwhelmed with her own worries to not see what he was doing.

Yet again Jackie warns her too not use him. But knowing it will fall on death ears. Jackie was paid what little she will give her for 3 hours work. She goes home to take a nap. Between the smell of the place. And her always talking as she was trying to correct the mess caused. The man who helps her do it too. But when she does it will be okay until she runs to him again and finds again. He is block on this newer laptop. But angry with Jackie for blocking him from using her accounts to pay for things he is having placed into his own 5th wheel again. Jackie sees her slight younger lady coming to her. Lifts her up. She was saying I know what you need right now. She goes with her willingly. Even if she is carrying her. I am Linda my dear. Smiles to finally learn her name. She is hurrying to her place. With males wanting Linda. Linda is in heat. Needs this human to help her out of her heat. They were inside the motorhome. The males were telling her to open her door or else. She sees Ben and his males behind the males. She seals her door. When the males turned around. They could not find the door. It disappears. The males were trying to get away. But when there were more paranormal male police coming, they were leaving in cuffs. Linda smiles as Ben does a thumbs up. She is closing the curtains quickly and the windows. Then the vents were shut tight.

She turns to see Jackie was naked. She watched her pants and panties coming off. She tells her. I know how to handle you dear. All Linda could do is watch as she has her spread her legs as she stood there. She was crying out in need. This woman was making her excited. She was doing things no woman has done. Not even all the Goddesses could. She gave up her body to her talented Jackie. She was saying please Jackie let me have you please. She said, are you certain you want me to stop right now. The crash of climaxing right then has her saying please don't stop. It was a flood gate of repeating climaxing that has her nearly bucking from her intense climaxing. At last, she said. Let's go to my bed my Jackie. Yes, my dear. That endearment hit a cord in her bat ear fox/dragon cross heart.

At last, she hears. I need to relax. She helps her lay down. She watched her grab her chest. Linda said I need to claim you quickly. She looks at her. Yes, please hurry. She claimed her Jackie. The pain was easing. But she makes a call to Sandy. Doctor Sandy are you home. Yes, Linda said please hurry to my space. She gives her the space number. She was told what was going on. Sandy calls the paranormal ambulance to meet her the space number she gives her. Sandy was there looking her over listening to her heartbeat. Any pain dear. Her name is Jackie. It's her birthday today. It will not be her death day is that clear Linda. Yes. Okay. How many time she has the pain. I only know of one. Sandy looks at Jackie. I am going to give you something for your heart. You place it under your tongue. She nods.

Sandy hears the ambulance coming to Linda's space. Sandy noticed the deep mating mark. Sandy looks at her friend Linda I asked permission. Jackie said yes. Okay Linda. They are what will help her. Sandy goes the door saw it was not one she has called. She rushed back inside. Quickly seals the door. Ben, I called for a paranormal ambulance. But it's not an ambulance at all. I rushed back inside. I am already making them get out. You stay put. You will need to see if the real one is coming. We have a human with a heart attack. I know who she is. Okay the real one is coming. I know the two coming. Good thing you did notice. It wasn't the right one. They must be listening for calls like this. The one by Linda's was clearly not an ambulance at all. It was too clear it was a lab van. The men in the van were jerked out quickly. Arrested and taken to a van.

Ben was driving the van to his driveway. Was going through it. Saw men from the RV park waiting for anything that he might place out on the ground or table. They jumped when several men in police cars came. They were in a trap they made by thinking they could steal any evidence around to sell. But they were getting a ride to jail instead. They were told you going to spend time here. Each time you are caught looking to steal something. You will get more time here. Their wives were looking for their husbands or boyfriends. They knew where they were heading. Ben saw the women coming. Tower talks to them. They went back home. Knowing they would have to handle things. For now.

Ben was glad she had come. Please can you take this van to your station. He sees a tow truck backing to where the van was parked. Hi Babe, what's up hot thing. You be careful your mate will probably want to spank me. She is out of the tow truck. She pins her to her hot body. Gives poor Tower a wanting kiss. With Tower moaning as she gives her one back. She marks her. Told her mark me you sexy female. Tower does. Babe tells her. She is your alpha to you too. When she learns Tower was not mated. Babe told her she has a tow job to be picked up. Tower said she was the one at the crime scene. Now Tower found herself mated to one dam hot female who knew how to treat her mate in her bed. Babe was showing she was the one now pregnant. Tower will be soon.

When Ana saw Tower return to work, she was signing out. Ana noticed she was marked by a certain female. She has seen Babe with the same one. She walks up to Tower. She finally caught you I see. Tower said, who? Okay play coy. I know that mark. Babe has the very same one. Blushing then grins. Yes Ana. She made it noticeably clear. She was going to have me. You need to be mated. Stop chasing tail to bed them. You love having young. Yes, I know I will be the one who will be having them.

She was gone before Anna could talk to her about moving in with her and Bumba. When Ana was telling her what Bumba had plan. Baby she is mating as we chat. No, it can't be. Yes. She belongs to Babe's mate. Babe is pregnant by her mate. Anna was crying. She has wanted her for herself and Bumba. Ana holds her. Why are you crying. I wanted her mama and Bumba thought we should. Baby you know how it is dear. Yes mama. Tower gets a workout with that female. I know. You don't think I have an attachment to her? I think every female around wants that beautiful female. Bumba came running to her mate. Loyal as always. Mama-in-law why is my mate crying. Did you punish her for something. She takes Bumba into her lap. Baby she is upset. Why? Tower is mated. She was crying too. We wanted her. Baby she was caught by Babe's mate. Oh, I see she wipes her was a tissue then she did it for her big baby. Tower is hers girls. She is that type as we know can be single mind. And she was with her mate when she may it noticeably clear she wants Tower. She will be a busy female now. Not jumping from bed to bed.

Biker Operation

Hey girls will you please come here. Yes Denise. Time to head out. I feel we will find a hot older woman. She turns around watched a hot woman running to her. Help me up please. She is off and placing her on her own motorcycle. Happens to see why she was wanting on her motorcycle. Girls on your motorcycles. We have trouble coming. They are also looking back. See another group coming up fast. Denise yells operation: Hot Stuff.

They spread out after Denise and ten other females with their own playmates. They were protecting their leader and her new mate. She was heading to the paranormal hospital. Denise knows she has a hot author on her motorcycle. The other biker gang knows it too. Please can you go any faster. Denise whistles loudly. She takes off. The rest were whistling. More of their friends join them next. Time, they make it to the paranormal hospital it was 100 strong. The smaller gang was staying on their tale. Then they see they are being blocked by 85 bikers. They were hot Goddesses and shifter females. The smaller gang was forced to return where they lived.

They were planning on finding her. Not knowing she was going to be with her honey she loves. Denise was kissing her Kate deeply. Denise, I want you now. She was lifted carried to the waiting bed. Kate I am so glad you got out of their hide out. It wasn't easy my hot werewolf. She was taken quickly by her Denise. She was working her up to making her claim mark. She has her so many times. But they wanted this more than anything. Knowing that the women from that biker gang will not see she has changed. They will be looking for the mature older woman. She was looking at herself in the mirror after she turned. She was giggling to see how much she has changed. Her Denise was holding her from behind. You are so hot my beautiful mate. She was taken for hours before Denise noticed she was going into her heat. Her was wonderful as a lover to her in heat body. She has taken her each time. She was so excited how she was making her the one pregnant. Denise was drawn to her not long ago. She was running to her motorhome. Saw the hot Kate as she was coming from her mailbox. Knew she was a dyke. But she had to have her help. Please my dear. I need to get inside before I am caught. By them. Kate had seen them. She takes her keys. Helps her inside. She was whining for her to take her out of her heat. Closing her door. She tells her to push the control by the door. It was sealing fast. Kate was covering the front window. Runs to shut the windows and curtains too. She had to jump on a ladder thank god it was out so she could. Denise was needing her to help her quickly. Kate was helping her to her bedroom. She was undressing her quickly. Then undressing herself. Denise was licking her lips when she was coming on her bed on her knees. She was spreading Denise legs quickly taking her fast. Denise moaning as she was taken out of her high heat. She was relaxing. With females in high heat, they go into bad pains and tense up their body. They are not safe when they are in this condition. Kate was taking her so gentle yet fast. She was out of her high heat. They can be hurt badly if the one who takes care of them in the high heat.

Males like to get a Goddess. They all dream of doing it to them. The males were still trying to get to Denise. One had climbed the ladder to the roof. He was finding he can't force the vents up. He was growling loudly. Anna was coming home for lunch. Bumba was off that day. She was busy in the Kitchen. Anna was ambushed. Kate said. You stay inside. The female next door is in trouble. Please be careful Kate. I will. She was after the males.

They did not know the heavy root was a weapon. Bumba was whining for her mate. Then a new female risked her life. No, she isn't. She was wanting to help her mate. But Anna told her. Stay link to me my Bumba. Ana was on her way with half the paranormal females with her. She knew she was going into danger. But that was her child they are trying to take.

Ana sees a gutsy human hitting males so quick and hard. They were going down and not getting up. The woman was not letting the males hurt Anna, she sees her birth mama was trying to get to her. Rocky was rushing at the males as well. Rocky, was working to save her friend Anna and then her own mate was in trouble. She was grinning at the gutsy woman. They high 5 each other. Rocky saw what she was using. Rocky was looking around. Saw the right branch she can use. Together they work to save the two who were too important to the females around the world. Anna was trying hard to keep her clothes on just like her mama was doing. They watch the human and Rocky knocking out the males. Ana noticed that they were thinning out.

Denise's braves coming out when Kate was taken by biker women were trying for her only. They had captured her and rode off with her. You be safe my Denise. Denise was pulling her motorcycle out from her motorhome. Anna and Ana saw what Denise was doing. They ran to get on their motorcycles. They all checked to be sure their back storage was shut and locked. Bumba and Rocky were on their own motorcycles. With several other females. They will not let the biker chicks win. They had not been gone long. But they did not know what they would face. Or how determined Kate was to be with her Denise. She tasted that hot dyke. She needs her to be hers as she knew she was already. Kate was placed in a small room while the women play poker to see who will have that hot older woman first.

Kate was working the window open. Using the sound of them playing for her. She was soon able to get the window open she was out and running. The women hear motorcycles. They run to see if she was still on the bed waiting to be taken. Not only was she gone. But she had found her clothes. She had dressed and slip out of the window. She found a milk carton up where she can slip down with ease. She was running when she sees her Denise has come for her. She was helped on the motorcycle.

They were riding to get away. With Ana, Anna, Bumba and Rocky. Plus 9 others. Soon there were so many. They were having the 15 go ahead as they slow down the biker chicks. They were not pleased to lose that hot mama. The leader was going to claim as her old lady. But she has not counted on the women she was fighting to protect were now helping to save her.

Kate was a sexy female now. With many thinking of her as a hero. Anna and her mama were so pleased with her. She was going to the large auditorium. They have just been let out of the saferoom. To find they were going to have Kate made a Goddess for her help to save the High Goddess and her Second to the High Goddess. Kate was blushing as she sees so many glowing females waiting for her arrival. Denise was already a goddess. Seeing her mate so honor made her so proud. She went out to do what Denise could not do yet. But she was gutsy. Now she was standing by her mate.

Sandy as Frist to the High Goddess came quickly. She was standing by Anna. Mina was also standing with her. And as Third to the High Goddess. Denise steps forward with her mate. Denise sees only love from her. There was a party right after. A blessing of knowing that that two were happy to be safe among their Goddesses. Their world was changing. Yet they seem to have the blessings of the old ones that went before them.

Now a new Goddess to the ranks that was told she will be known as the protector of her Goddess sisters. They all cheer her. She was indeed a protector. Her weapon was taken before it was stolen. It was on display. A mark of what all were taught. She was teaching all the Goddesses her style with the weapon she had used. They were all in awe of how she used it.

Kate will find she will have to protect Anna again. It was a week later. She was getting out her car. Placing the roof up on her car. When two men not from the RV park had come behind her as she was snapping the roof into place. Kate was walking from the dumpster. She was on the attack swiftly. Anna was soon joining her. She told Anna how to hold her weapon. Anna was doing what she has told her. She was doing it the first time. A van pulled up to help the men being hurt by the two females. But found they were hurting them. They were falling fast. Ana was coming back from the store saw a van in front of her big girl's motorhome. She texted helped needed Anna's. There were so many now beating up the men.

The doctor was watching from another van. He was now loading his dart gun. He wants the hot woman helping the other female. He was leaving the RV park. But he was shocked to see the hot woman in front of his van. He said, come here honey. She can smell deceit from him. He was trying to find the dart gun. He found it. She was quick as he was aiming the dart gun in her direction. She slammed her weapon down on his arm. She watched the dart go off as she hits his arm. She moves in time to save Anna. Anna was falling from a blow to her head. The man who had shot the dart gun was hit hard on the top of his head. She was beside Anna she was up running to the hospital with many females following. Sandy saw her coming fast. That female can sure run. She was seeing was, Anna was clearly hurt. She tries to keep up with Kate. Sandy growls show her to room one hurry. Anna is hurt.

Even the 3 other vans could not keep up with the female. They lost track of the one who was carrying the one they had to take to the lab. All the Goddesses were running to get to Anna. They were inside the whole building went to lock down. Alarms only the females can hear was heard.

They were rushing to the safety of the paranormal building for females. There was a secret way into the building. They were coming fast and getting inside. Red Lady Ops females were helping them. There were a lot of vans all the same with C.E.M. Labs they had come to collect as many females as they could. But going for Anna was the biggest mistake. With the one female who will step in and be her bodyguard. The vans were driving around to find all the known females in the location. The one who was protecting Anna was on the top of the list. Anna was second on their list. They do not know who they are dealing with. She was out on the hunt.

The men were being killed and the men had no protection. Denise was worried sick. She goes to find Ana. Knowing Anna has a bad bump on her head. It was her mate who had saved her again. Then she was gone. Ana was following the female after the men who set this up. She did not know she was on the top of the list. She had found it out by going through one of the vans. Kate was laying a trail the crime units were waiting as she was killing and moving on. They were telling Ben. She is after another van. I can't see how she is doing it Ben. What does that mean male. How she is killing them. Dam she is another assassin I see. She keeps saving Anna. She was fast that any car can go. Anna is being seen too. Have you seen Ana. Ben said, no why. She has not responded to her cell or her police radio. Simply great.

That female was after the men, but she was following the dam sexy female as she was attacking with something that conceals herself. Ana noticed she is working fast. Ana cannot believe there is another assassin in their Goddesses. She was able to see how she was doing it. She whispers be careful Ana. Moves just in time. She watched this female kill them and tells her to stay close. She will not be please to lose her too. She was learning by watching as Kate was still on the path she has taken. She was the protector. She earns the title. She was waiting as one was looking to find a place to pee. He went into the alley but will not come back from there alive.

Another went to find him. They needed to get back to the place the females were staying. He first whispers. Are you finish Mac? Nothing. He walks into the alley. He was dead before he fell to the ground. Ana finally saw what she was using. Dam it, she just understood what she was. She was smiling. Then a whisper goes to the right behind the dumpster. Stay there. She does. Seeing two men from the van. Ana heart was beating so fast. She was so dam lucky she was protected by this assassin Kate. She noticed she has been called several times. She has the sound off. She sees several text. Where are you, Ana? Denise said, Anna is getting better. Please tell me are you with my mate. Hiding the cell screen, she said, she is about to kill two more. You wait until we are done. Tell the rest. To stop draining her cell battery. Okay.

Anna saw the first man choked then the second was. Then she sees Kate go to her. Follow me whispers in her ear. Dam it. Her whisper has her so wanting. She must clear her head. And good thing they had moved from the alley. A hungry male was looking in the dumpster. He smells two females were here. He was sniffing found humans dead. Then he sees the crime unit that clean crime scenes. They throw him their dinner. He leaves with the food. They collected the 4 bodies. They were back on the trail of the two females. A female that was doing the sniffing was Rocky. Tracking her mate and Denise's mate. She was grinning knowing when Kate whispered into Ana's ear, she was shaking her head. No doubt to clear her head.

They sure were moving fast. They see Kate was back on her path. Found the driver sleeping in the front. Three others were talking to the whores on the street. They were laughing when they see a sexy woman then another going to driver side have the men watching them as they did something to the driver. They were able to get the men to go with them. Men have their brain in the wrong place at times. The men were going to have the whores. Even have their pants down getting taken by them. He was wrapped up in what the whore was doing to even hear a woman behind him. The woman was giving him what he asked her to do, was moving fast when the other woman with the other woman told her to leave. He had his eyes closed. She was running back home. The man had no time to react to save himself. He was dead. Kate with Ana following her. Were at the next man was being taken as well. The woman sees one was behind the man she is up and running home too. He was dead quickly. They can hear the other man telling her take it like tell I told you bitch. She sees the two women behind him. He was not pleased she has stop. He was killed before he was going to hit her. Like her friends she runs home. Back on the trail of the vans and the men that were looking for them.

The men from the last location were collected. Rocky was directing the male where to turn. He was good at his job. He respects Rocky. She had saved his sister once. She was a happy mated female. She was going to have her 5th litter. He was looking forward to more nieces to spoil too. He sees the two they have been following he said. We will need to stay here doctor. It's too risky. They watched how fast Kate had manage to kill 12 from 3 vans parked. Even Ana was shocked how fast she was working. She tells her it's nearing sunrise. They found the last van. The men were relaxing, and they were all sleeping. She moves quickly. They were gone within 10 minutes.

Rocky was out of the crime unit cleanup van. And runs to her mate. They were kissing. Kate said, follow me quickly. The sun is coming up. She has her car waiting. They get inside race away from the location. They were all inside the hospital. Going to see Anna. She was sitting up. Smiling at Kate. You female are very skilled it seems. Ana goes to her big baby. Looking at her head. It was a good thing what they used wasn't like Kate's weapon. Female are you a trained assassin. Yes, my dear. You are the high Goddess I am going to keep you safe female. Anna tells her. You were on the first and I was the second. My birth mama was the third. Her mama was shocked.

My dear no matter where I am placed. I am to protect you. She looks at something she always wears. Tell me where you got this, she touched it. She was looking at her with a clarity. You can't be. Yes, I am Anna. Ana touched it. She was crying. She was held by Kate. Rocky came to them she touches the thing she wears. She was shocked. How it is possible. I carry her likeness as her because I am hers, she had me I was taken away in time. Bumba comes to check her mate with Sandy following. Sandy sees something she knows all too well. You are my baby. Yes mama. When I was taken to safety so you could be the doctor you became. I protect Anna. Yes, we have been hearing what you were doing with your alpha mama following. Anna looks at her mama and Sandy. Ana was holding her love child she had given her. They were not mated at the time. Anna said, please come to me my sister. She does. She smiles yes, my big sister. You were my sister all this time. How is it I did not know it. It wasn't to happen until I saved you several times my sister. Is it true you outran all the cars trying to keep up with you. You carried me all the way to the hospital. I can go faster. Anna was smiling at her. I want to see how fast you can. Kate, Anna is good at running. I will take that challenge my big sister they shake on it. When may I be release from here. Sandy said, we do have a track here you do know that female.

Yes. I use it all the time. They were letting Anna get dressed. She walks to the track showing her sister where she works out. They were stripping down to their panties and bra. Ana was smiling to see her girls getting ready to race each other. Sandy was smiling to see her baby racing Anna. She smiles at Ana. As she raised her right arm with a towel. She said, get ready. Go. They watch both racing each other. Sandy saw her face in Kate.

Ana was seeing the same view. They both were racing so fast it was only a flash of bodies racing. Ana was using the gage to see how fast they were going. Sandy was grinning as they came around for the 12th time still going. Ana said time. They were needing to sit. They were grinning at each other. Rocky goes to check out Anna then Kate. Water please Bumba. Bumba was so please with her Anna. She has 4 bottles. Drink it slowly girls they smile. Together they said, yes mama. Rocky was giggling. Denise comes to see her mate and Anna both in their bra and panties. Saw the sweat from both. Then hands both a big towel. She looks at Sandy then her mate. She said, Sandy? She knew what she wants to know. She is my baby from Ana. Looking at Ana. She just smiles. Our love child. Okay. Ana could not help laughing. So, who won the race. Both did. It was a tie. Okay. Okay my mate, are you ready to handle your mate. Or do you have another assassin job. All the females were laughing. Denise had said it, as if it happened every day. Ana said, my girls need a workout with their mates. Mina walks into the room. Hi Kate. Hi step-mama. You both have a race? Yes, a tie. Good. Time your birth mama was home for her workout. This time Mina did it without a hint of sounding upset. She just asked in a way that has all the females grinning at her. They went home with their mate stayed busy for two weeks.

Cargo Drivers

She Is One Hell Of A Driver

Be careful Colleen. I will mama. Her mama always worries for her big girl. She is so dyke. Women love her. But cross her. Watch out. She is the only woman for one Cargo company. She is hard as nails when she must work around men. They like her. But know she is all business at work. She sometimes hangs out with them. Women not sure about her. But Colleen has a tender side. She is a bit older than she is. She has a body with curves she wants. Sam watched as Colleen walks up to her. Gives her a kiss that makes her mush. You ready baby? Depends on what's in the offering. Collen kissed her. Hearing her moan. Colleen you want me I see. Yes, you sexy woman I need in my life fully. She lifts her arms. She is lifted. You ready my tiger. She makes a soft tiger sound in her human ear. She giggles. You did it again my tiger. Good. I want you to be my strong human.

She carries her to her rig. Then picks up her orange Maine Coon cat Helena. You can come too. Colleen shuts and locks Sam's motorhome. Walking back with Helena's dishes and cat food. She eats meat she is given by her tiger mama. Colleen loves her shifter girlfriend. No other can drive her needs to be handled like her Sam can. She only wanted Sam after the way she has her from the first touch. Sam please. Yes, my love. She is after her again. Making her so needy for her to make love to her again. Her smaller tiger was very protective of her with other females getting too interested in her love she wants. She is a little person/tiger shifter. They both want it. Colleen gives her the right to claim her. Getting her excited and lusted up. She takes her big sexy dyke as her mate. Helena is sleeping in Colleen's driver seat as they mate. Colleen was happy now she was off work. They go to the paranormal safe room. Colleen was bobtailing that day. She pulls into the back of the building.

Colleen's mama calls her. Baby where are you? At the Paranormal hospital mama. Did she? Yes, I asked her too. Can you have visitation by your mama? Mama, why? Well. What mama. Um, I am hum. I think I like to see if I can draw a female to me child. Go through the police station. Walk carefully. Do act like you are looking. See what happens. Oh, play hard to get. To a point mama. Okay. I am game to try it. She parks behind her child's rig. Goes inside. She was heading upstairs when she was being watched. She was a beautiful woman big like her child. She was approached by the Captain. She smiles at her. Hello my dear. Are you lost honey? I was hoping to see my child Colleen. She is with her smaller mate a tiger. That has Lonnie getting closer.

Connie was breathing in an excited way. You alone honey. She said, yes Captain I have been for a long time. She licks her lips. You need a woman with werewolf. She watched her getting closer to her as they were nearing the stairs. Lonnie why haven't seen me before now? She was kissing her deeply. Touching her body in her secret places. Because I am waiting. Waiting? Yes, I must get you trying to get away from me. She watches Lonnie relax she slowly moves and then she ran up the stairs. She can hear her coming fast. She keeps running and was inside the hospital. Sees a friend. Hiding behind her. Lonnie was grinning as Anna stepped away. It was enough time for Connie to run to a room Anna told her to go.

Lonnie was running into the room. She is smiling. Connie was taking a shower. Connie knew when she was getting in the shower with her. Hi, Connie. Hi, yourself Lonnie. Turning the bigger woman around, she looks up at her Connie she was the faster female. Chasing Connie was exciting. Anna was told a friend was being chased by Lonnie. Allow it to happen. Now at last Lonnie is mated again. Connie was needing to be with someone.

Connie was on Lonnie faster than she was ready for. Lonnie thought she be the stud in this relationship. She was looking up the beautiful woman looking into her eyes. Daring her to challenge. Lonnie loves the way she has her on the bed. She is being undressed fast. Understanding she wants her to take the alpha role.

It was always going to stay that way. They were rushing to the hospital to have their young months later. Dodging medical vans. They had been warned. They were doing a lot of zig zagging. And said, we need help. They are trying to box us in. The males were on the medical vans tail. More came just as Connie drove pass. The vans were hit from the side. The vans were not able to move. The men were mad as hell. The doctor was badly hurt. He was paralyzed from his waist down.

He was crying. Please help me out of here. I can't feel my lower body. He was told you will be out of pain now. The shock from the burning then pain was unbearable. He was dead. One said, how many do you think he has killed. No one knows.

Christiana Hills Loves

It is said, she was a lover to so many in her lifetime. Rumors some say. She has them in her mind. She will not talk to anyone. One nurse keeps her full of drugs. She goes to her at night. Takes her body more. Leaves before she is catch. Draining her each time. She is helping herself. She is nearly caught the next night. She slips out of the room. Rushed from the hospital. She is stronger now. She has more she must take from her. She will be dead soon enough.

She sees what she fears. She was laughing. I will drain all her body. You are too late to help her now. Assassins were there to capture her at last. The second wraps her up and carries her to her doom. The first walks into the hospital right to Christiana Hill. Mama I am here. She has terror in her eyes. She has drug me child. I fill like I am being used as a straw. I am feeling so weak. I am taking you from here. Say nothing for now. She nods. As she carries her adopted mama from her room. A nurse was telling her she is not allowed to leave her room. Where are you taking patient 103. She has a name bitch. The nurse ran to get the doctor. He was with another patient. Nurse patient 60 needs a diaper change. Please doctor. What is it. I have barely started my rounds. I have a golf game at noon. Patient 103 is being taken out of the hospital. Not on my watch. Get the diaper. Yes doctor. He was running. All he saw was a woman leaving. Saw no patient with her. She was laying in the back of the car. With a light blanket.

Sandy, I have found my adopted mama. She has been drugged she was being drained of almost all her blood. We know her blood type. Her sweethearts said, to tell you thank you for finding her in time. She was pulling into the police garage. She sees Rocky waiting. She lifts her best friend up and carries her to the room was made ready for her. She was placed asleep by Anna. She was so stressed to see this beautiful woman made a meal for a vampire. She was being drain of the blood she has drunk from her victim. She was saying it's my blood you are throwing in that bin. Shut up bitch. Both assassins were with the female vampire. She was not looking at the second. She fears her the most.

She hears her say. Go be with your mama. I can handle her. Thank you. They are cleaning her blood of the drugs she was given. She was feeling the ones she had love coming into the room. Sandy said, my dear. I have all the females you have ever loved, here for you. She said, doctor am I am going to have them as well. Sandy was giggling. If you want them. They are giving you, their blood. Oh, my goodness. You girls are going to be able to look at me insides. They were laughing. That is our girl talking. Sleep now. She was in a deep sleep. Bumba watch for any problems. Yes doctor.

Days later she was sitting up and chatting with her lovers. She was blushing as they come to her. You should decide dear. She looks at all. Must I have to choose? I want all if given that right. They all were grinning. You heard her doctors. She was taken to the safe room. She was bouncing on all of them. She was so wonderful to their bodies.

Come Where I Am Waiting Woman

The much older woman was afraid to go to this younger woman. She isn't sure why she will want her over the younger beauties that live where she was living. She is facing 70 in a few weeks. She was finding her around her a lot. Always coming inside as she was sleeping. She has her sleeping naked. She has her keys to her travel trailer too. she was taking her body as she was laying there wanting her when she was there. But not wanting her life so controlled by this beautiful woman.

She was getting more needy for her touches each day. She was wanting her to take her again. She was soon made his mate. She has her now. She was watching as she was getting young after she has claimed her totally. She was looking in the mirror at her baby. She is seeing she will be having her young too. she was getting aggressive with her younger mate. She is giving herself to her now. It was a game of aggression for each other.

One day a male came to take back his younger mate. But found an older female guarding her closely. She told him to leave, or he would pay. He laughed in her face. She attacks him so quickly. She was in and out quickly. He had made the mistake to meet her where she told him to go. She knew how to fight any male for what she has. The younger female has made the right choice when she had her ready to take her and kill the male who forced her mama and had killed her. he had this younger female caged one day he made a mistake. By not locking her inside his house. She had gone to find the right woman she knew would kill him one day.

She was so happy she had made this woman what she was to become one when she will not remember her soon. She is going back to where she truly lives. She was ready now. But for one more thing. She has her make her pregnant. Then she leaves her the house and the jewelry behind. She will have her young back on her planet. Her now dragon will need to seek a dragon to breed with the continue living on as she is now. She will find a true beauty wanting her soon.

Shade's Tempting Body

Cold Winter

Hurry everyone inside the cabin right now. It is getting colder. Two were collecting firewood. They were looking for something to get it started in the fireplace. It was a while before they found the matches to start it. They would keep it running throughout the night. They were looking for more wood to help keep them warm.

Amelia has Susy's hand. They disappeared into a back bedroom with their sleeping bags. They zipped them together. Undressed quickly. Both getting into the sleeping bags together. They were kissing each other. It was getting hot and heavy. Then they were finding ways to get each other all night. It was too warm in their sleeping bags. They could not help it. They were taking each other at the same time. They were quickly back in their sleeping bags. Susy was spooning Amelia. She kissed her neck. They were sound asleep.

Alex has Andie with her. They had stayed by the fire. They were driving each other wild with the way they were after the other woman. Egging each other on to see who can make the other wild with need for more. Andie was louder than Alex. They had moved from the fire. Zipping their sleeping bags together. So tired after enjoying each other. Andie wanted to spoon Alex. By morning Alex was spooning Andie.

Elle was sleeping by herself. She opens her eyes when she feels a draft. Sees Sam zipping their sleeping bags together. They smile at each other. They were soon kissing tenderly at first. But they were soon wanting more from each. Sam was more aggressive. She takes Elle fast. Driving her need higher to have her take even more. Elle was working up the nerve to take Sam. She was after Sam the rest of the night. Sam was excited by how Elle was making her body feel.

May was chasing Sally. She finally caught her. She was giggling as May was kissing her. Playing with her breast. May, I need more. Yes, I know Sally. My hand is wet with your cum on my hand. Yes, you are driving my need higher. She was moaning as she was sucking her breast. Arching her back as she was sucking her nipples. They were perked to have her take them more with her sucking them. They fell asleep holding each other. May wakes feeling Sally kissing her. Sally. Yes, May. You were wonderful. So, are you May.

Nancy sees Anita walking to her. She looks into her eyes. Are you sure? Yes, Nancy. Taking her hand, they disappear into the only other room left. Nancy was giving herself to her friend. She has wondered if she would want her or not. She has had a crush on her. They were so happy to at last to take each other.

In the morning they heard a key in the door, doorknob turning. They all run to get dressed fast. The door opens. Girls you here. They come from the rooms grinning at her. Yes ma'am. Good. Please help me with the groceries. They were outside bringing in the food. Sorry I was not here last night. She has a big box of wooden matches. Shade sees the firewood is needing to be filled. Girls, please bring in more firewood. They were watching as she was bending over. God she is built. Shade has heard them. Shade goes to help them with the wood. She was having them help her lift them. Shade carries more than they can. She was wearing only a tee shirt. Her super-size breast drew their eyes to them. Smirking at them. You like them girls. They nodded.

Going back into the house Shade is undressing and goes to her shower. They were undressing chasing after her. Shade takes her time. All 10 were in the super-size shower with her. Shade was touching each. They were touching her hot body. Shade was loving their touches to her werewolf body. They were wanting to taste her pussy. Shade opens her legs wider. They all tasted her. Shade has had many women at a time stay at her place. Know they would take their friends the night before she came the next morning.

Shade takes each again. They are all lusted up from her talents to them. Agreeing to be hers. She used this cabin a lot. She will take them home soon to be her mates. They will stay with her for not the 300 years she normally would. When she let them go find another mate to love. Start over with new women. For now, she will love them all deeply. They were always wanting her body even more after they turn. Shade was skilled with their bodies. They learned a lot from their hot alpha mate. Shade was being teased at the paranormal women police station. She was noticing that her mates were needing new mates. She found suitable females for them. They have seen her talking to several females one night. She would tell each one. I have selected good mates I can trust to love you as you are used to having. They hugged her went to their new mate. They were all lifted and taken to the female's homes to live a life with only one female.

Moving On

To claim the one woman, Shade has wanted from the first moment she had seen her. It was clear. Waiting for the 300 years she normally has her mates was impossible to wait. She must claim her. She has never had a serious need to want just one mate. But she was getting older, and she will not risk losing her at any cost.

Okay my dear friend I am going to have you soon. Shade was thinking about a woman she has been wanting to have in her bed only. Shade walks to her door. The woman goes to her door and sees the one woman she has had so many dreams about. Shelly allows her into her crowded travel trailer. You wanted me? Yes, my dear. Shade was backing her up to her bed. The woman was saying now. Yes, my dear. Shade watched as she takes her bra off. Shelly watched as this aggressive woman was shutting and locking her door. Shuts the window and the curtain in the kitchen. Shade was undressing as she was advancing on her. Shade watched as she was having to sit down to get her pants off. Shade sees a long scar on her left leg. Shade was helping her so carefully pull her pants then her sexy panties off.

Shade was over her now. You need my full attention darling? God yes. You are so hot compare to me. You are a Goddess my dear. Oh, my goodness. You are a sweet talker. This woman was not used to being told things positive about herself. Shelly watched as she made herself comfortable between her legs. Teasing her clit at first. She knew just when she would climax from her taking her clit. She was loving her sounds as she was making love to her pussy. Shade was smiling as she was bucking from her mouth making her climax over and over. She was the right woman for her. She was slowly getting her wanting whatever she wants with her fired up body. Not bad. For a gal of 67.

 Shade tells her I want to claim you as my mate, and you will only have to say yes. She was seeing the look in her eyes. She understood what she wants. I must have you for however long I have left to give you. She was claimed quickly. Her mark was very deep. She licks her neck. She was climaxing hard for her to suck out all she can give her. They both lay in her bed. So, Shelly could catch her breath. She was giggling. You sex on a stick. Thank you for making me yours. I am the one who is honored you said yes to me.

Going To The Safe Room

 Shade wakes her mate. Let us hurry my mate. We must rush to the safe room right now. Yes, my Shade. Shade had the room already set aside in case she had said yes to her. She helps her up on her Harley Davidson. Speeding quickly. Using her flashers with her mate hugging her as she did. She sees several vans. Using her radio. She yells over her engine. Several vans waiting on Main And Rogers. We got it Shade. What is your E T A? coming through the hidden location. I will alert the ones who need to know. I see you. Bring your motorcycle in now. Seal going down. She gets off her motorcycle helps her cherished mate.

They walk inside. While Shade pushed her motorcycle as she has her hanging on to her as she does. She has found her life mate. She will never leave or give her to another. She was being extra careful with her prize. She has never wanted a woman or female this much to be so protective. She sees her mamas waiting as she comes through the station she works at. They were walking behind her as her protection. They did not need to be asked to do it. Their big girl was showing she was going to settle down at last to just one. Seems she has learned to accept she has found what she has needed. As a child of two Goddesses, she was given time.

Now she was walking with her. They know of the woman. They like her. She is one who can spend a tales to have you feeling you were in the vision she was seeing as she was writing the tales. They were at her place. Cleaning it up. She clearly spends her time writing not on cleaning as much as she might have done. They take her old dog for a walk. He sure was sure interested in them. Shade's birth mama was in heat. He was learning to behave. He was taken to be fixed by Sandy. He was calmer around werewolves they did notice. Sandy just smiles at him. He was given a trim. His mama was always writing. She looks after them and tries to keep up on his grooming. Sandy had no problem understanding she was a busy author. Considering how many she has done in over 5 years.

Sandy keeps him awhile. When Rocky came into the room, he was staying she placed out food and water. He ate and had water. She walks him so he can go potty. He was treated special by the doctors and nurses. He licks her face. She growls at him. He sits down watching her. She grins. Now you listen male. I am taken by my mate. So, no doggy kisses. Her Ana comes into the room. You gave my mate a doggy kiss boy. He wags his tail. She bends he gives her one. Now that was okay. But no more my grandson. Your great dame Rocky is not into doggy kisses. Rocky was looking at her Ana. Do we have to be his grand dame? Of course, my dear. Oh, good here come the girls. Rocky was fixing them next. Two beautiful females. She was glad the male was already fixed. Shade was a Goddess. She asked her mamas to make her mate a Goddess.

They see the cats and the dog. Shelly was on her knees. Her pets all four came to her. She was hugging them she noticed her dog was groomed. Looking at her mate's mamas. Thank you for looking after their needs. She saw her two girls were fixed like her dog. It will be a lot quieter in our home. She was looking at her hot mate. She looks like both her mamas. Child, looking right at Shelly. We cleaned up your place a bit. We know your mind is probably more focus on your books. Thank you, mama-in-law. Welcome child. Shade wants you to be a Goddess like we are, and she is as well. With tears her eyes she lifts her alpha mate. Making her giggle from more the shock she could. The kiss she was given has her moaning with need for her to take her right. Ana giggles. I think they need to get back to have fun. Come girls. You too boys. Her pets go with Ana. Rocky was rushing to her next operation. Ana walks back downstairs to her Chief office. The cats and dog stay in the office with her. There was a cat box for the cats to use.

Every time they went in its Ana was quickly cleaning it out. She would just smile say my grandchildren had to go. She walks to the dumpster to throw it out and return. She was able to get her work done. They would peek out the door. Bobtail worked up the nerve to walk out to where the females were busy. He went to a tiger shifter. May was totally surprised he was in her lap. She could see her a fix male. So, she allows him to stay in her lap. Ana was rushing around looking for her grandson. Has anyone seen my Bobtail grandson. May giggles. Are you Bobtail he was wanting to be picked up. She grins at him. Getting him to allow to lift him up was so easy. She walks with her buddy. Ana sees a look on May's face. Her picked my lap to sleep on Ana. Looks at the big tiger holding him so protectively.

Ana was grinning at her. You big softy. She grins. Before returning Bobtail. She kissed him he licks her face. Made May giggle. She smiles as she hands him to Ana he was purring as she too kissed him. She was given a washing on her hand. She was falling for this big cat that was a loving cat. When he went out of her office the next time, Ana went to see if May had him. She replied not this time. They were both looking for him. Soon all the females were looking for him. He was going up the stairs looking for his mama. With his half-sisters staying up with him. Ana was smiling. She was staying up with all 3 she opens the door to go to the hospital part. Bobtail was a direct path to where mama was.

 Shelly was getting taken by her mate again. She was sure making so many exciting noises that has so many wanting this exciting female too. Shade sees her mama signing her cats want in the room May was carrying their cat box. She was trying to hold her breath from the smell. A cat shifter said, let me have that cat box female. I am used to the smell of cat boxes. May looks at the smaller cat shifter. She meows at the cats. They meow back at her. Tell your child I will look after them myself. So, they can continue their mating. Ana turns to see her. And she was talking to them. Ana follows her. Rocky sees her new nurse taking charge of the 3 cats. She sees them go to her. The cats rubbed up on her legs. Sees her Ana grinning at her. You are their doctor my mate. Good thing he is fixed too. Nurse. Yes, doctor. After you are finished. Please see to your family. Yes, doctor.

Ginger was waiting as she has the cats go into the room she has set up for her own sisters. She sees her mama having more sisters. She had asked the older cats to watch over them. She was helping her mama with the delivery. May was excited by this tabby cat female. She was watching her so much she opens the door. May slips inside. She was spending time with the tabby cat female she was so intriguing to watch. Ana had to go get May. She has her by her left ear. Ana told May. You are working female. She goes back to her desk. May was going to go see her on her lunch time. May no female. Ana tells her firmly. May was not pleased to be told no.

Ginger came to see May. Gives her a kiss as a cat will do. Ana was watching like the rest. Ana comes to May's desk. Okay if Ginger wants you as much. I am going be there to help you in any way I can. To see you both happy. Ana sniffs Ginger. She was lifting Ginger and carrying her and half dragging May. You handle her female. She is in heat. No wonder you want her. Clear she wants you. I want to be their God mama. May hugs Ana and she in the same room as her mate's family are. She was yowling now she was in full heat.

 Her mama watched the tiger being so gentle with her oldest. She has mated with a bobcat female. Ginger was a lot bigger than her tabby mama was. But she was not told she was a mix of tabby and bobcat. Rocky knocks on the door. May allows her inside with Ana coming inside. Ginger was calm for the moment. When she was told she was a tabby/bobcat mix. She was grinning. Now knowing why, the bobcat was in their life. She was asking to be with her mate. She makes a bobcat sound to be heard by her tabby cat. She meows to have her allowed to come inside with her. She sees her big kitten was a full female with a tiger as her mate.

As they were watching the last of the big kittens Rocky was checking them all. May was in the kitchen taking her mate more. Ginger is a demanding female. May was having so much with her mate. Ginger was after her much bigger mate. Making May so excited her own way of taking her. May was sure climaxing a lot from her ruff cat tongue. She makes her bigger pregnant. May had been so careful to only give her only a few. They would develop in Ginger then be transferred to May to carry to term.

Shade's Tempting Body

Cold Winter

Hurry everyone inside the cabin right now. It is getting colder. Two were collecting firewood. They were looking for something to get it started in the fireplace. It was a while before they found the matches to start it. They would keep it running throughout the night. They were looking for more wood to help keep them warm.

Amelia has Susy's hand. They disappeared into a back bedroom with their sleeping bags. They zipped them together. Undressed quickly. Both getting into the sleeping bags together. They were kissing each other. It was getting hot and heavy. Then they were finding ways to get each other all night. It was too warm in their sleeping bags. They could not help it.

They were taking each other at the same time. They were quickly back in their sleeping bags. Susy was spooning Amelia. She kissed her neck. They were sound asleep.

Alex has Andie with her. They had stayed by the fire. They were driving each other wild with the way they were after the other woman. Egging each other on to see who can make the other wild with need for more. Andie was louder than Alex. They had moved from the fire. Zipping their sleeping bags together. So tired after enjoying each other. Andie wanted to spoon Alex. By morning Alex was spooning Andie.

Elle was sleeping by herself. She opens her eyes when she feels a draft. Sees Sam zipping their sleeping bags together. They smile at each other. They were soon kissing tenderly at first. But they were soon wanting more from each. Sam was more aggressive. She takes Elle fast. Driving her need higher to have her take even more. Elle was working up the nerve to take Sam. She was after Sam the rest of the night. Sam was excited by how Elle was making her body feel.

May was chasing Sally. She finally caught her. She was giggling as May was kissing her. Playing with her breast. May, I need more. Yes, I know Sally. My hand is wet with your cum on my hand. Yes, you are driving my need higher. She was moaning as she was sucking her breast. Arching her back as she was sucking her nipples. They were perked to have her take them more with her sucking them. They fell asleep holding each other. May wakes feeling Sally kissing her. Sally. Yes, May. You were wonderful. So, are you May.

Nancy sees Anita walking to her. She looks into her eyes. Are you sure? Yes, Nancy. Taking her hand, they disappear into the only other room left. Nancy was giving herself to her friend. She has wondered if she would want her or not. She has had a crush on her. They were so happy to at last to take each other.

In the morning they heard a key in the door, doorknob turning. They all run to get dressed fast. The door opens. Girls you here. They come from the rooms grinning at her. Yes ma'am. Good. Please help me with the groceries. They were outside bringing in the food. Sorry I was not here last night. She has a big box of wooden matches. Shade sees the firewood is needing to be filled. Girls, please bring in more firewood. They were watching as she was bending over. God she is built. Shade has heard them. Shade goes to help them with the wood. She was having them help her lift them. Shade carries more than they can. She was wearing only a tee shirt. Her super-size breast drew their eyes to them. Smirking at them. You like them girls. They nodded.

Going back into the house Shade is undressing and goes to her shower. They were undressing chasing after her. Shade takes her time. All 10 were in the super-size shower with her. Shade was touching each. They were touching her hot body. Shade was loving their touches to her werewolf body. They were wanting to taste her pussy. Shade opens her legs wider. They all tasted her. Shade has had many women at a time stay at her place. Know they would take their friends the night before she came the next morning.

Shade takes each again. They are all lusted up from her talents to them. Agreeing to be hers. She used this cabin a lot. She will take them home soon to be her mates. They will stay with her for not the 300 years she normally would. When she let them go find another mate to love. Start over with new women. For now, she will love them all deeply. They were always wanting her body even more after they turn. Shade was skilled with their bodies. They learned a lot from their hot alpha mate. Shade was being teased at the paranormal women police station. She was noticing that her mates were needing new mates. She found suitable females for them. They have seen her talking to several females one night. She would tell each one. I have selected good mates I can trust to love you as you are used to having. They hugged her went to their new mate. They were all lifted and taken to the female's homes to live a life with only one female.

Moving On

To claim the one woman, Shade has wanted from the first moment she had seen her. It was clear. Waiting for the 300 years she normally has her mates was impossible to wait. She must claim her. She has never had a serious need to want just one mate. But she was getting older, and she will not risk losing her at any cost.

Okay my dear friend I am going to have you soon. Shade was thinking about a woman she has been wanting to have in her bed only. Shade walks to her door. The woman goes to her door and sees the one woman she has had so many dreams about. Shelly allows her into her crowded travel trailer. You wanted me? Yes, my dear. Shade was backing her up to her bed. The woman was saying now. Yes, my dear. Shade watched as she takes her bra off. Shelly watched as this aggressive woman was shutting and locking her door. Shuts the window and the curtain in the kitchen. Shade was undressing as she was advancing on her. Shade watched as she was having to sit down to get her pants off. Shade sees a long scar on her left leg. Shade was helping her so carefully pull her pants then her sexy panties off.

Shade was over her now. You need my full attention darling? God yes. You are so hot compare to me. You are a Goddess my dear. Oh, my goodness. You are a sweet talker. This woman was not used to being told things positive about herself. Shelly watched as she made herself comfortable between her legs. Teasing her clit at first. She knew just when she would climax from her taking her clit. She was loving her sounds as she was making love to her pussy. Shade was smiling as she was bucking from her mouth making her climax over and over. She was the right woman for her. She was slowly getting her wanting whatever she wants with her fired up body. Not bad. For a gal of 67.

 Shade tells her I want to claim you as my mate, and you will only have to say yes. She was seeing the look in her eyes. She understood what she wants. I must have you for however long I have left to give you. She was claimed quickly. Her mark was very deep. She licks her neck. She was climaxing hard for her to suck out all she can give her. They both lay in her bed. So, Shelly could catch her breath. She was giggling. You sex on a stick. Thank you for making me yours. I am the one who is honored you said yes to me.

Going To The Safe Room

 Shade wakes her mate. Let us hurry my mate. We must rush to the safe room right now. Yes, my Shade. Shade had the room already set aside in case she had said yes to her. She helps her up on her Harley Davidson. Speeding quickly. Using her flashers with her mate hugging her as she did. She sees several vans. Using her radio. She yells over her engine. Several vans waiting on Main And Rogers. We got it Shade. What is your E T A? coming through the hidden location. I will alert the ones who need to know. I see you. Bring your motorcycle in now. Seal going down. She gets off her motorcycle helps her cherished mate.

They walk inside. While Shade pushed her motorcycle as she has her hanging on to her as she does. She has found her life mate. She will never leave or give her to another. She was being extra careful with her prize. She has never wanted a woman or female this much to be so protective. She sees her mamas waiting as she comes through the station she works at. They were walking behind her as her protection. They did not need to be asked to do it. Their big girl was showing she was going to settle down at last to just one. Seems she has learned to accept she has found what she has needed. As a child of two Goddesses, she was given time.

Now she was walking with her. They know of the woman. They like her. She is one who can spend a tales to have you feeling you were in the vision she was seeing as she was writing the tales. They were at her place. Cleaning it up. She clearly spends her time writing not on cleaning as much as she might have done. They take her old dog for a walk. He sure was sure interested in them. Shade's birth mama was in heat. He was learning to behave. He was taken to be fixed by Sandy. He was calmer around werewolves they did notice. Sandy just smiles at him. He was given a trim. His mama was always writing. She looks after them and tries to keep up on his grooming. Sandy had no problem understanding she was a busy author. Considering how many she has done in over 5 years.

Sandy keeps him awhile. When Rocky came into the room, he was staying she placed out food and water. He ate and had water. She walks him so he can go potty. He was treated special by the doctors and nurses. He licks her face. She growls at him. He sits down watching her. She grins. Now you listen male. I am taken by my mate. So, no doggy kisses. Her Ana comes into the room. You gave my mate a doggy kiss boy. He wags his tail. She bends he gives her one. Now that was okay. But no more my grandson. Your great dame Rocky is not into doggy kisses. Rocky was looking at her Ana. Do we have to be his grand dame? Of course, my dear. Oh, good here come the girls. Rocky was fixing them next. Two beautiful females. She was glad the male was already fixed. Shade was a Goddess. She asked her mamas to make her mate a Goddess.

They see the cats and the dog. Shelly was on her knees. Her pets all four came to her. She was hugging them she noticed her dog was groomed.

Looking at her mate's mamas. Thank you for looking after their needs. She saw her two girls were fixed like her dog. It will be a lot quieter in our home. She was looking at her hot mate. She looks like both her mamas. Child, looking right at Shelly. We cleaned up your place a bit. We know your mind is probably more focus on your books. Thank you, mama-in-law. Welcome child. Shade wants you to be a Goddess like we are, and she is as well. With tears her eyes she lifts her alpha mate. Making her giggle from more the shock she could. The kiss she was given has her moaning with need for her to take her right. Ana giggles. I think they need to get back to have fun. Come girls. You too boys. Her pets go with Ana. Rocky was rushing to her next operation. Ana walks back downstairs to her Chief office. The cats and dog stay in the office with her. There was a cat box for the cats to use.

Every time they went in its Ana was quickly cleaning it out. She would just smile say my grandchildren had to go. She walks to the dumpster to throw it out and return. She was able to get her work done. They would peek out the door. Bobtail worked up the nerve to walk out to where the females were busy. He went to a tiger shifter. May was totally surprised he was in her lap. She could see her a fix male. So, she allows him to stay in her lap. Ana was rushing around looking for her grandson. Has anyone seen my Bobtail grandson. May giggles. Are you Bobtail he was wanting to be picked up. She grins at him. Getting him to allow to lift him up was so easy. She walks with her buddy. Ana sees a look on May's face. Her picked my lap to sleep on Ana. Looks at the big tiger holding him so protectively.

Ana was grinning at her. You big softy. She grins. Before returning Bobtail. She kissed him he licks her face. Made May giggle. She smiles as she hands him to Ana he was purring as she too kissed him. She was given a washing on her hand. She was falling for this big cat that was a loving cat. When he went out of her office the next time, Ana went to see if May had him. She replied not this time. They were both looking for him. Soon all the females were looking for him. He was going up the stairs looking for his mama. With his half-sisters staying up with him. Ana was smiling. She was staying up with all 3 she opens the door to go to the hospital part. Bobtail was a direct path to where mama was.

 Shelly was getting taken by her mate again. She was sure making so many exciting noises that has so many wanting this exciting female too. Shade sees her mama signing her cats want in the room May was carrying their cat box. She was trying to hold her breath from the smell. A cat shifter said, let me have that cat box female. I am used to the smell of cat boxes. May looks at the smaller cat shifter. She meows at the cats. They meow back at her. Tell your child I will look after them myself. So, they can continue their mating. Ana turns to see her. And she was talking to them. Ana follows her. Rocky sees her new nurse taking charge of the 3 cats. She sees them go to her. The cats rubbed up on her legs. Sees her Ana grinning at her. You are their doctor my mate. Good thing he is fixed too. Nurse. Yes, doctor. After you are finished. Please see to your family. Yes, doctor.

Ginger was waiting as she has the cats go into the room she has set up for her own sisters. She sees her mama having more sisters. She had asked the older cats to watch over them. She was helping her mama with the delivery. May was excited by this tabby cat female. She was watching her so much she opens the door. May slips inside. She was spending time with the tabby cat female she was so intriguing to watch. Ana had to go get May. She has her by her left ear. Ana told May. You are working female. She goes back to her desk. May was going to go see her on her lunch time. May no female. Ana tells her firmly. May was not pleased to be told no.

Ginger came to see May. Gives her a kiss as a cat will do. Ana was watching like the rest. Ana comes to May's desk. Okay if Ginger wants you as much. I am going be there to help you in any way I can. To see you both happy. Ana sniffs Ginger. She was lifting Ginger and carrying her and half dragging May. You handle her female. She is in heat. No wonder you want her. Clear she wants you. I want to be their God mama. May hugs Ana and she in the same room as her mate's family are. She was yowling now she was in full heat.

 Her mama watched the tiger being so gentle with her oldest. She has mated with a bobcat female. Ginger was a lot bigger than her tabby mama was. But she was not told she was a mix of tabby and bobcat. Rocky knocks on the door. May allows her inside with Ana coming inside. Ginger was calm for the moment. When she was told she was a tabby/bobcat mix. She was grinning. Now knowing why, the bobcat was in their life. She was asking to be with her mate. She makes a bobcat sound to be heard by her tabby cat. She meows to have her allowed to come inside with her. She sees her big kitten was a full female with a tiger as her mate.

As they were watching the last of the big kittens Rocky was checking them all. May was in the kitchen taking her mate more. Ginger is a demanding female. May was having so much with her mate. Ginger was after her much bigger mate. Making May so excited her own way of taking her. May was sure climaxing a lot from her ruff cat tongue. She makes her bigger pregnant. May had been so careful to only give her only a few. They would develop in Ginger then be transferred to May to carry to term.

Drive Your Rig To My Company

She has a friend check out the company. I had not told the man anything about me. I used a cheap phone paid just enough minutes to make the call. She drove to the address. Saw what she thought might be a trap. Took several photos. Talked to a good friend. They had reached out to someone else. They raid the place. Found several women were chained to beds. They were being used. It was a front to get trucker women to fall for the ad. When they showed up with their rigs. They were ordered out their rigs. They were dragged to a house chained to a bed. The rigs were sold off. But the one they were hoping would come sounded so sexy. They had men rushing to have her the moment she was ordered out of her rig.

Going Back in Time to The Ice Age

Why Must I Go

Why do you want us to travel that far back in time? She was slapped. He said get in this machine bitch. She does. She was in shock. She had been snatched from the street. Thrown in his car. No one will miss her. She will be the first he will make travel so far. She was feeling the machine was moving. It stops. So fast she was thrown from the machine. It was gone quickly. She will never be able to return home. She worries about her pets. She must find a place to get out of the rain. She found a small place. She was digging to make it bigger to stay. But she was forced to find another place to stay. She wanders all night.

By the early morning she was sleeping in a tree. The rain had stopped. She wasn't a young woman. But she has no way to go back to the time she knows best. She was getting down when she saw white cave lioness following her as she tried to climb a tree when a mastodon walked too close to her. The cave lioness was on the attack, the mastodon moved off. She looks at the beautiful cave lioness. She walks up to her. The cave lioness stands her ground. Reaching with no fear. She runs her fingers along her back; she has a thick coat of fur to be able to survive this ice age. She watched her laying her head on her back. She straightens saying my back is hurting. I know you don't understand me. But you saved my life. Thank you honey.

 She was going to try some berries but was pushed slowly away from them. Holds her back as she is guided to a cave. Taken to sleep on a bed. It was the female's bed. She was an early shifter. She knows this beautiful woman was her mate. Catherine was sound asleep. Turning into her human she undressed this woman very slowly. She wants to taste her. She licks her clit. She hears her moans of pleasure. She sees she likes it when she licks her there. She gets so excited. She must take her now; she claims her quickly. This time. They did not ask if they wanted to be claimed. She was awake when she was turning into a cave lioness. She looks at the female she watched closely. She walked up to her as she was growling at her. She sits down and waits. When she came at her. She only moves out of her way. She was quickly learning from her mistake. But she will help her understand why she had to have her.

She went hunting, brought back her kill to share with her. She was so hungry she was watching her drop the meat. She watched her go after it. She was eating it all. She leaves quickly and returns with more. She brought the meal closer. She eats what she can. She was returning with the last part. A male has come to her cave. Wanting the female as his mate. She was standing guard of her meat and not letting him near her. She can smell she has gone into her first heat. The male saw the female he fears of all around. She was backing off. Smells the rest of her kill. He was eating fast. But he is not aware two were there together. He was killed quickly.

Looking at the female she goes to her. Starts washing her face then she was rubbing up on her. She helps her to understand how to return to her human. She helps her out of her heat. She was even louder as she was being loved by her mate she now understands. They are leaving this cave. They travel in their cave lionesses as it was getting worse to travel in their human. They would check for a new cave to live in. Some were just for a night.

They soon see others not fully human. They would travel with them a while.

They were soon finding so many humans like them, but they can smell their animals as well. They were approached by other females that like others like they do, her mate was finding she was being approached a lot. Her mate was leery with them. She was the one who was protecting her younger mate. But when she saw they wanted her instead. She clearly knew how to defend herself quickly. Her mate watched and learned as they are now staying in their human. They had clothes as they had to look like humans more and more. They were invited to stay at different lodges made of different materials. Because they were women, they were always welcome. But men found out quickly she was letting them know she was not interested in them. She and her mate would thank them for allowing them to stay. But felt it was best to leave. The head woman in one place would take them to her bed instead. This powerful woman wanted her, and she would take her mate as well. She has no man living with her. Her brother referred to his sister on this matter. They worked as a team. He has the men understand the women were now his sister's. The men still try for the older woman. But found out how the head woman leader felt about it. She quietly told her brother. I must leave to protect my women. He helps to get what she will need. You stay safe my sister. Hugged. Tell our younger brother to take my place.

The men were drunk when they worked up the nerve to force the head woman leader to give up the older woman. Not even aware she and her women were gone already. She had been turned by the older woman She was not risking her mates. The men were following a trail rarely used. Saw 3-women footprints. Following them. The prints were gone all sudden. They walked a bit more and found nothing. The women knew they were being followed. Climbing into a tree in their humans. Not saying a word. Watching as they staggered around. The men finally gave up. Return to the lodge.

Waiting a while to be sure the men would not return. They climb down from the tree they all had climbed on. They run from the location. Catherine looks at Kona her first mate and Ano her second mate. We must decide where we should go. They found a cave with no one living in it. Not even an animal of any kind. Ano works out a plan for them with their leader, their mate Catherine helping with her modern thinking of her own time.

They worked well together. Hunting bigger game. Leaving extraordinarily little behind. Always on the move. They find a cave to stay in winter. Catherine was restless. Ano tried to convince her to settle down. But she has a feeling she will meet her new mate. She tells her mats to stay if they wished. She broke her bond. She travels the lands on her own for 6 mouths when she found her way to a cave.

Time Travel Mishap

How did I get to this place? Joy was looking at a new item in the museum. It said stay off. But she had to peek inside. She sits in the seat. Was playing with the controls. She saw the door shut. Simply great. Now how do I get out of here. She touched a control by the seat. She watched as it was going backwards. Now she was in a panic. She feels it moving. When it stopped there were no numbers any longer. The door opened and she was ejected from the seat and out the door. She watched it disappear. She was in a cave of some kind. She is looking at a beautiful naked woman. So, you were brought to this time too. She is alone. Catherine waits as the woman stands up. Hi, you hot looking babe. She looks at Joy boldly. Come to me my dear. I will help you understand.

Catherine made the cave her home. Hunting sometimes when she felt like it. She knew she was to meet a woman from her own time. Joy walks to her. She was kissing her all over her powerful body. Catherine was enjoying how aggressive she was being. She gives her body freely. She tells her. Please undress. Joy does it quickly. Catherine was on her hot body. Now Joy was crying out as she took her body. I want you Joy. but I am going to tell you about me as I keep taking your hot body. Yes, please take my body.

Like Catherine was when she was tricked to go with a cruel way with women. She was her age. But she no longer looks like she had been. They stay on each other for hours. Tells her to dress. It was getting chilly. She was so into Joy. She forgot she needed wood to keep the cave warm. She went to get more. Joy wants to her hot woman. She was hers all the way now. Giving her mate the right to make her a cave lioness. They were going to her stash of firewood.

Catherine tells her. Tomorrow will have to collect more. They return to the cave. Catherine was growling low. She found the animal who was looking for her food she keeps cold. The she was on the animal so quickly. It was fighting for its life now. But this female was too skilled in hunting thanks to her two mates she sent away to live together make young with. Catherine had not wanted to have young. They seem to know it.

Joy was watching from her mate how to hunt as her animal needed to do. The day a small herd of Mammoth herd came through. They had their first taste of baby Mammoth meat. Joy loves watching her beautiful mate hunting. She was watching her dragging it back to their cave. She goes to help her. Together they have it inside. She tells her let's eat our fill.

They were just moving the bones to the high shelf when Catherine hears a sound outside. She rushed in her cave lioness. Smells it is her two ex-mates. She calls her mate to help with them. They were in their human. They turned into their humans. Brought them to the fire. Catherine is helped to cover the mouth of the cave.

They rushed back. They were needing her doctoring right then. She has her mate help them while she rushed to get what she needed. They were undressed. But were pregnant. Could not help each other right then. They needed her help. With her new mates help they were able to help them deliver all their cubs. She was looking at the small helpless cubs. She sees her mate having the females turning into their cave lionesses. They watched as the cubs begin to nurse their mamas. She was finding food to help them to able to give them enough to keep making milk for their young. The females were starting to feel so much better with Catherine and Joy helping them.

Catherine had bulked up and her arms were powerful than when they had seen her last. She was working out in a corner. She saw 3 females watching her working out. She was ready to go hunting now for 4 females and she had been training her mate how to hunt too. They were bringing in the meat. The nursing female stayed with their own young. They were both watching Catherine a lot. But knew Joy was her first mate.

While out hunting Joy talks to her Catherine about them. She wanted to know if she will take them back. Catherine looks at her Joy. I have been wondering how you would feel about it my mate. They need you too my Catherine. Yes, I can see that. You are the first mate. I am glad you wanted to talk about it with me. They dragged two baby Mammoths back to the cave. They were twins. The Mammoth female was stuck in a big crack of ice and not one of the older females of the herd, could help her from her death trap. They had to continue to a warmer spot to graze and keep their own young safe.

They drag the two Mammoths inside. They were licking their lips from the smell of fresh kill. They see Catherine was hunting for them. They soon understand that the gift of baby Mammoth was her way of saying she will have them back as her mates. With Joy as her first mate. They were smiling at both. They saw where the knives were now kept. They were seeing the skill she must make them.

She watched now her adopted young were growing fat on their mama's milk. They were soon back in heat. Joy was at the same time too. It will happen when women or beast lived together, they will go into heat at the same time. Catherine was no different. She was needing help to get out of heat. All 3 of her mates take her together. She was out of her heat quickly. She was an alpha with 3 mates. She was after all of them. Catherine makes all 3 pregnant with her own young. After seeing the young cubs, she wanted to help make her own.

She was back hunting for her 3 mates and even her older cubs in her mind. She was out every day. She brings in the meat. They were making it ready to freeze. Using the bladder after it was cleaned completely. They process the meat. Made new places to store the meat. The back of the cave was the coldest place to store it all. They would have their young in a baby crib strapped to their backs as the collected other food items the human body needs. Catherine was bringing wood to store up for the next winter have an equal number of different kinds of foods.

Catherine bringing in all kinds of birds, there were many smaller animals to hunt. She was at her hunting place when she smells a woman running from three smaller wolves. She rushed them. She had told her where to run and stay. She is ordered to cover her eyes. She does as the sexy woman ran back down to where the wolves were smelling the human. But find a powerful cave lioness waiting for them. They knew her to well. She was on the attack quickly. She collects them decides they can use them too. She had not damaged their fur. She was back in her human. Okay dear. Follow me. She does. This beauty was suntan and stronger than any woman she has seen. She is told to stay calm and talk quietly.

Walking into her cave she was watching 3 other women with young. She was being careful. She must wait for her eyes to adjust the difference of lighting.

Her stomach was growling. She was hungry. Joy saw the 3 wolves were now dead. Their mate was a very protective female. She was asking Ano to find her clothes. She was smiling. Come my dear. Following the woman to the back. She found something she can change from.

The Pride Was Growing

Denise was becoming so interested in her mate she was told she would be hers completely. When she was taking her, her other mates were feeding their young in their cave lionesses. She was used to them doing that each time. She was helping Catherine to deliver the cubs. Earlier that early morning. Now Catherine was taking her 4th mate. Denise was happy to be hers completely a few hours later. She turned into her human in the back of the cave. She was back in her human once more. She was taken again by her alpha mate.

By the next day Catherine was out hunting for her growing family. She cannot believe her luck to have so many females. She drags a large deer back home by herself. She had to take breaks to get it back near enough to butcher it. She is dragging the parts she did not need to a place she would so other meat eaters could have. It was an old buck. Pass breeding age. The rack he had on his head were the largest she has been able to bring down. She watched him trying to win the females. But his time to breed was ended by the younger buck. He was in runt and the older male had been. He did leave many females with his own young. Her females were helping to take the meat inside. One was watching the young as their mamas helped their mate.

Denise was happy to watch all the young. She was telling them stories she was making up. She was making places to store the giant deer meat. She was giggling when she sees her shared mate being fitted from the pelt of the deer. She needed more room for her powerful body. She was allowing her the time to make sure it will fit her right.

They were comfortable inside the cave. The hide had been replaced. The old one was used in the back of the cave to make the area colder for all the meat their mate has been able to bring down. Knowing her 4 mates and young will need it. She was watching her mates one day. Thinking about finding a new cave soon. It was getting crowded with 5 grown females and their young.

She was gone for one day. Returns with even more females to look after. As her mates help them, she is telling them she has found a larger cave. Not far but it was clearly being used by a different kind of people. She was not finished. But they do not hunt here. Catherine was checking out a cave that will work best for her growing group of mates. They were wolves that asked her to allow them to be with her and her females. She has seen them several times watching her when out hunting. She knows they had travel back in time to find her. But seeing she was not alone. They go with her. They had the outfit they needed for this time period. They helped them hunt. Bringing in wood to keep this cave warm. They were staying in their side of the cave. Letting Catherine her mates not have to feel they were too close to their family. They were clearly all mated and not looking to take her large group of females.

When Catherine was taking time out and just looking for something to eat. Her first mate brought her some of the fresh meat she and the wolf female helped her bring in. They were a big help. She was warming up to them. She goes to talk to the one who was clearly the leader. She was talking quietly with Anna. She told her. About finding out how she had ended up in this time period. That her first was also find the same time. Catherine smiles. Said, she was the one I knew who was coming. I was waiting for her to come. Even had broken her bond to her second and third mates to have her. She was looking at this female.

You are missed by so many my dear. The man was found and questioned by a male we trust. He told him what he had done. Is he gone. So, I can feel safe if I can return. I will not leave my females and young behind here. I am theirs I love them all very much. Yes, they are going with you and yes, he is dead. Your fans have been worried about you. Oh? Yes, when you disappeared, we were on the hunt to find you. You have been gone so long. But your fans wanted you found. That includes all of us as well.

Seeing that sexy smile has Anna feeling a need she can only think is the time when wolves were having to find a mate. She is so alpha. Bumba was kissing her Anna. She smiles at her mate. Thank you, my loyal mate. Catherine asked. Why do you glow so much. We are all Goddesses. Will I change back to what I was. No, you will be the female you are. Anna hears a sigh from her. Good. How is it you can travel back in time and return. We as Goddesses have that ability.

You and your mates and young will be leaving tonight. Your safety and your family have become dangerous. Males are heading here to claim you and take your mates. Will kill your young to have every female ready to breed. We need to go. Our hard work. Is not as important as your lives are. They leave carrying young and other things they wanted. They are told to hurry into the plane. They do. The plane has the controls now. Anna said, back home. Hurry. The plane takes off and she is going forward in time back to the time they needed to go.

When they reach their time, they wanted. Anna takes the control back from her loyal plane. The females were looking at the time as a crowded place to be coming to. They watched how their mate and the first mate were smiling at all they could see. They were looking forward to a hot bath. A real bed. They were giggling at how things had not changed for them.

Anna tells Catherine your large house is waiting for all of you to live in peace. Anne lands on a long runway. She noticed her mama was waiting for her plane to stop. She was so excited to see her and Bumba back. Rocky was by her side. How much do you think she has changed Ana. I had not thought about that.

She was watching as her big baby is leading a large group of females to the limousine. Rusty was waiting for them. She sees her old girlfriend was so hot looking. She was sleeveless her arms looked hot. She sees her Rusty looking at her hotter body. She tells her mates to go inside the limousine she wants to talk to her lover. They do as she request.

Their talk turns into a long kissing moment. She was saying to Rusty. I never thought I ever be kissing these lips ever again Rusty. Please tell me. Rusty whispers I am single. The moment I heard you were being returned to me I broke my bond. I cannot break my bond my love. I am not asking you to do that. I want to be yours too. She tells her mates. She is the one who I was in love with before I was thrust back in time. As I told you. But not about her. I hope you all will understand she is wanting to be my mate too. They all had been holding their breath. But let it out knowing she will not be taken from them.

Anna was watching the reactions of the females. All they care about is not losing their mate. Anna goes to her mama and Rocky. They both hug her then Bumba. You were gone so long baby. We had to be mama. We are all back. Ana hugs all the females who had gone with Anna and Bumba.

They follow the limousine to where Anna has arranged into a home for Catherine and her mates and young. Anna had called on the way to the house to get a lot more beds for her young her mates have. And adult size beds. She has three freezers packed full of freshly hunted meat. Ana had been busy hunting with Tower, Rusty. And few others. Ana had announced that Catherine was returning to her writing of her books. Her fan base was so excited to know she was back.

Hauling Tractors For A Living

She has been doing the hauling jobs. Hauling tractors of all sizes. She loves doing it. At first men did not like her doing it too. Now she is the one with so much skill after 30 years. She was out for a good time with a woman she is hoping anyway. She was finding herself on a sexy woman's lap being given a hot kiss. She was so into her attention to notice anything or anyone. She had a date with this hot older woman who was going to have in her wanting. She was walking her to a limousine. My rig is parked at the truck stop. I am being driven to her estate. I am being taken again. She has taken me twice so far. I have not had a woman look after me like she has. She has made it noticeably clear she will have me as hers.

 My rig is driven to her place. My trailer is on it. I had quit as she has requested, I do. I love how she wants me this much. My rig was being serviced as I was in the shower first then her bed for two days. I was served my meals in bed by her. I am so surprise how she wants me so much she is spoiling me so much. She had asked me to take her now. I was on her so fast. She was getting excited by my way of loving her body. She was saying yes baby you are what I really need.

I had gone to check on my rig. I was pulled into the garage where they had finished my rig's necessary repairs done. She tells me. You are being misled. She has plans you will not be able to control your life after she claims you as her doner. I asked what that means. She must have your body fully and then she will take your will to think for yourself. Here are your things. And money you will need. She is sleeping in her coffin. As you probably know she never sleeps with you. Yes, I had noticed that. I am being directed how to get out of the location. Told to change my phone number quickly.

I sold my rig as well as my trailer. I have learned my mistake with her quickly. I had nearly lost my soul being misled by her. By her finally allowing me the right to take her at last. I had gone outside for some fresh air. I had woken wanting something. But I see someone in the room. Holding a finger to her lips. Then was given my keys. We were rushing to my rig. She told me what I had been laying with. I was feeling scared I had gone to bed with a vampire. She gave me a number to call. She was going to be leaving. Knowing she could be killed for taking me from her. She was not waking up. The High Goddess came. She saw her asleep. The one who made a point to save me had given her all the information. Even the tainted blood she gave her.

Anna killed the vampire with a lethal drug made only for vampire. The scream that came from her was loud. Anna was being protected by her mama. She was her backup. The Timberland special forces were their extra backup. She will be burn right after along with her home. The two women were being seen. I was waiting my turn to be seen. I was naked being looked all over. I was reaction to their eyes checking my body. I have no bite marks from her thank god. She was going to make me like her the next time she was coming to take me again.

The other woman was helped to forget her. She was looking so scared of her own control she had on her. But she was not totally. She was used to a point. But she needed her to drive her where she wanted her to go. When the vampire saw me, she was hungry to make me hers. I was so flattered to be taken by the beautiful woman I thought anyway. To learn I was the easy mark she needed. Once I am cleared, I was taken to get a shower. I was being given a hot shower with a true beauty. She was dark and so sexy. I was reacting to her teasing me like she was. I was begging her to take me. She was on my needy pussy. I was bucking her hand right about then. She was smiling. Big mama you sure love what I am doing. I am saying through my teeth with a hiss. Yes honey. You are making me want you to have as yours forever. Good. Because that is what I want you sexy trucking mama. Your rig is now replaced for an upgrade. You and I are following Anna the High Goddess. You want more darling. May I have you too. Of course, my dear.

Anita is holding her hand. They walk out of the shower going to safe room together. They did not seem to care if they were naked. Clothes were washed brought back to where they were going to be staying all night. They were too into each other but each other. Anita was happy she was given her sweet lady she has wanted for so long. Always watching her hot body. The woman was so sexy in her own way. Anita had been searching for her.

She was talking to friends when she came into the club. Saw her leaving with someone. When she learned she had been saved in time, she begged Anna to let her have her. Anna saw a look she should know from this female. She has been without a mate. Always mooning over a woman, she had no idea who she was. Now she sees her walking to her. Anna heard Anita has a human she was clearly in love with. Anna had to find out who she was. There she stood with Anita. The woman who had been saved. She was glad she had not been bitten. When a female wants a certain woman or female Anita did. It could kill the Goddess too.

Hello My Love

I was supposed to meet a raven-haired woman. As I wait in the line to get inside the door of the club, I am sure being checked out by a beautiful woman looking at me. She is a raven hair. But is she the one I was to meet? She is coming to where I was standing. Hello my dear. You are lovely. Thank you. She said something she had read from her Facebook friend. She was moaning when she kissed her. You are the one I was seeking and now that you are here. I wish you to be with me.

We danced all night. She was kissing me so much I was having to calm her leopard down. Easy baby. If you want me then we should go, get a room. She licks my werewolf ear. I was moving fast. I have both of us outside. Do you have wheels female she was licking my face. The motorhome by your pickup. I am lifting her. Running like hell. Give me your keys. She does. I am opening her door. Told her to hurry quickly inside. Shutting and sealing the door. She is in full heat. She was climbing on me as I am closing her windows and curtains. I am ripping her clothes off. She was making her leopard in heat sounds. Drawing so many to the motorhome. I hope I can reach a friend. Hello Kay. What's going on. I am with a high heat leopard. I can handle that. Pickup is at. Giving her the address. She said you go slowly out the driveway. I have a group of paranormal police females coming now I will get your pickup back here. Thank you. You better take the female here. Okay. Yes, you can speed to do it. I will clear it. I am driving slowly as she is licking my neck.

I see the paranormal police. All females. They sign we will be following to be sure you get to the hospital. My alpha mama was grinning wide. She was going to having a leopard as a daughter in law. It was just my alpha mama and myself at the alpha house. The pack were always out looking for a conquest. She has a certain human to find. She was on her timeline. Saw she has accepted her friend request. Not wasting time. She text her. She was sending her a photo. She was finally seeing who she wants in her life. She sends a phot back. They were talking so much now on video chat.

How Do You Dance?

I was wanting to dance at this new club. I see another cute woman just coming inside. I am a lonely grizzly needing to find a sexy woman to make happy. She sees me looking at her. I noticed no one even paying attention to her. I was though. She was my type. She goes to sit at the next table. She has a look of hope. I clear my throat. Honey may I sit at your table. She turns and gives me a hot toothless grin. I am waiting for her reply. She signs yes please. I am intruded with her. I sit down across from her. she sees a look she has been needing after a rotten day. Losing her job. The new boss was so shitty to her. Just because she uses sign language. Her voice was so throaty. Women were wanting her. So, sign language was her way to talk. She is looking at this bigger woman paying attention to her. she was not looking away. She signs, As she spoke to her as if she were as normal as anyone. Well, she was. Her throaty voice was getting her too much attention. She was going to be this way until the one she would want can see pass her sexy voice.

If You Will

It's late and I am so tired. I have done all I can to make like I wasn't here.
They have told me to ready. They will be taking me right in my bed. I am
crying when I hear a soft voice. Let me come in and hold you. I looked at
her from my kitchen. I wipe my eyes. She said, get your wallet keys place
your cats in carries. I will take your

I WANT TO CLAIM HER AS MY MATE

Tiji has no idea I am always following her around. That ass she has is heart
shape. She swings it in away her limp is barely noticed. She is heading
inside the club. Her ass swings more when she goes inside. I am close. I
can tell she has played with herself. She must know it alone has turned
several beauties watching her. I know if I don't claim her fast, I will lose
her to Goddesses. I am on her so fast and taking her to my motorhome.
She looks up at me. She has a wide grin. She has a look I have wanted to
see. She tells me. It sure took you long enough. You wanted to claim me I
bet. I am lifting her up so gentle. Taking her to my motorhome. I rushed to
shut, lock, and seal my door. I am over her older body. She has undressed
as I was dealing with my door.

I see trust from her. She was wanting me to take her now. She pulls me to
her. Said, kiss me.

They Only Think I Am Too Old

I walked into a club I used to go to. I noticed a lot of younger
women. She was about to leave. The bouncer lifts her up. She walks
upstairs. I am confused. I am in her apartment with her. I asked.
Don't you have the door to watched. It is being watched. I saw you
getting in line. I knew you might leave. But I wanted you so much
my dear. Me? Yes, my dear. She was bringing her closer to her.
Gives her a kiss. That has her moaning loudly. I thought so. They
were laying now on her bed. Lee was close to her age. She gives
herself to her after that kiss. She was removing her clothes fast. She
has her own off. I want you as my girl honey. As she was Taking her
left breast and sucks it. Causing her to moan. Oh, god, woman you
are driving me crazy with need. You want more. Yes, don't stop. She
is smiling as she takes her right breast next.

I was hoping you had a need for someone in your life my dear. Have since I dumped almost 4-month relationship. I did her a lot. Finally let her have me. But you let me have you. You my dear were the aggressor. That had me fired up. Oh, yes. I am needing your dyke to take me more. It's just what Lee wanted to hear. The Goddess Dyke has wanted her a lot longer than she could know. Lee was with her Sammi all night and she allows her to take her as her mate. She was taking Lee. Lee was loving her attention to her own body. Having another Dyke taking her was driving her wild. This was the one she has dreams about for years. When she took off as a lesbian author driving her wanting her to the point to wait for only her to take her body like she was right then.

The High Goddesses had wanted to help with her heat. But could not let her do it. She always taken her more after that. Anna had been at the club following her and Lee would have to go into hiding to keep her from wanting her as her plaything. She was giving her body to her Sammi. They were not leaving the room. Lee had rush to get food in her place and then she saw her. Talking to her best friend. She is coming here. Okay. You go to the door play bouncer Lee. Thank you.

Lee was there as she was coming. The real bouncer smiles at her. Good luck. Thank you. She watched her looking into the place. Knowing why she had started to leave. All there that night was too young for her. Lee had decided to just lift her up and carry her the apartment she was staying for free, thanks to her best friend. It came in handy when the High Goddess came to the club looking for Lee.

Bumba was always glad Lee was hiding she would call ahead to the owner know they were coming to the club. And Lee would be hiding. Lee was sitting with her hot mate smiling at her a lot. The High Goddesses came in sees Lee. Made a bee line to Lee. She was shocked to see she was mated. She stood up. Hello High Goddess. Her mate stood up stands with her. Anna was charmed by the new female. Hello High Goddess. I am Sammi. She shakes her hand and shakes it again. Anna grins. My dear surprising how many don't shake hands. So glad to see someone does. It's rather refreshing. Then Anna smiles. You are the Author I have been reading a while. You do seem to know a lot of different subjects. I like knowing things. And doing research is important when writing a book. I never thought about that part.

Writing is my vocation in life. You seem to have found yourself a great one for your mate Lee. Good for you both. My mate and I have friends to go see. I like to see you again Sammi and your mate Lee. Perhaps soon. Yes, of course. Thank you for the invite. Bumba likes Sammi. She was an exciting woman. She saw the look in her mate's eyes. Anna turns to see the look she must have too. They left. Ana came next. May I sit with you. Lee was up and helping Ana sit. With Rocky standing behind her rubbing her shoulders. Are you alright? Oh, I am fine. My mate is my doctor. I am carrying a lot of pups. She said, I am pregnant with my Lee's. They were talking about their upcoming pups. They were talking about a lot. Rocky was talking to Lee. They are having a serious talk about Anna and should let her mate know. Anna was clearly wanting your mate. Lee was not pleased to know she might try to take her from her. She asked, Rocky to dance with her mate while she talked to Ana. And keep Anna away from her mate.

Lee talks to Ana about how her child has been wanting her and she been hiding from her. she spoke. She might be doing this to get back at her. Lee told Ana, how she had been relaxing for her mate to come to her. And she tells her how she had come and nearly left. Telling her about having to hide to keep Anna from taking her while she was in that state. Knowing she wanted her as hers. Telling her mate, she loves to have us come visit her and Bumba. They both wanted my mate. And the look they have in their eyes makes that clear.

Ana was troubled for Lee. The last time there was a fight with her baby. Nearly 80 years later it had taken to talk again and mend their relationship. She has been acting up a lot. She would return each time she had a feeling one of her old playmates from the past. Kept Anna returning to the club. The dyke Goddess was in heat and she couldn't find her. She was saving herself for the mate she has now. They clearly love each other very much.

Lee sees her mate running to her. Ana was concern. Rocky was next to run. Ana placed Rocky behind her. Lee did the same with Sammi. Anna was lusted up and wanted Sammi. Tower lifts Anna up carries her in her left arm. She sees the lust in Bumba's eyes too. She was given Bumba as well. It seems several of the Goddesses were going to handle them. Ana had been ready to defend her Rocky. Rocky was growling. Not letting her mate get hurt or have another fight with Anna.

Anna was taken her own motorhome and to the room. Bumba had no choice was taken in there too. The door was locked by orders from Tower. Tower had the skills to handle Anna. Anna was watching Tower. What she did has both Anna and Bumba both taking her instead of Lee's mate. She has placed something on herself that will wear off soon. By that time, they should be out of their lust. Sandy had made it. She made sure Tower would not get pregnant. Sue drove Anna's motorhome back to where they all live. Sandy had driven them to the club. Knowing this might happen. Anna was going with her mate to safe room set up for them to stay. They will have food brought to them. Dykes with the duty to keep them from getting out or going after anyone who came into the room. Anna was needing confinement and so did Bumba.

Anna was given a sedation and Bumba to be given it. Gene was examining Anna saw what she has seen in only dragons. Anna and Bumba have dragon too. She works with Sandy to help them. Anna was not happy to be stuck in the room and she has only her sweet Bumba to sleep with her. Both suffering from the same thing. They were after each other a lot. Ending up with both pregnant. Tower is back to driving her rig. Ana was told she must wait her big baby. She was having Rocky's pups. They look like Rocky. Ana was home as she was nursing them.

 Jinn-Lin was acting Deputy Chief. A human was working as the Chief. But she had issues about having none-white persons working at the station, she was being given the duty to keep the officers in line. By someone. Jinn-Lin did some serious digging. The human was arrested quickly. She was not the one assign to the station. Jinn-Lin ordered the officers to find her. She was found quickly. By Sammi. She was clinging to Sammi. The female was totally shaken by the ordeal the human put her through. They decide to take her as their mate. Sammi calls her mate. Lee joins her. They have a female to keep happy. Now she was able to go back to work. She was laughing with Jinn-Lin. They got along.

When the men came to take the females, they did not know the inside woman was already dead. The shields were down before the men could reach the building. Even the roof would be impossible to get onto. Spikes were waiting for the helicopter when it goes to land. It was damaged seriously. It falls from the roof. With all dead, on impact with the ground. 4 large vans had pulled into the parking. Thinking all the females would be easy to get into vans. The doors were wide open.

The vans have cuffs, chains, and ankle cuffs. With stun guns to knock out to combative ones. The doctors had come to help drug them if necessary. To find the woman who was to take all white to the vans. Found she had not done her part in hopes the top doctor would want her as his wife. She was almost a twin to the one the who was the real Chief. Jinn-Lin was too good at her job. The human did not know the job at all. And not aware how this group of females were.

The head doctor was not smart about shifter female policewomen. The ones in the station they targeted knew what to look for. The human was too busy trying to get the ones she felt were not what the doctor wanted. Getting them on the on patrol quickly as far away as was possible. And it was what has Jinn-Lin had her on total guard.

The Sins You Weave

Child you should be careful with that one. Why mother? I don't trust her motive. Your father wants you to stay at home. Mother why did you marry him? Sighing, please sit down. Okay. She waits to hear the truth at last. Look I was your age. I met your father at a after school party. I was naive. Still a virgin. He took me that night. I lost my virginity to him. He made a lot of promises. But then he found I was carrying his baby. That was you. I was told by my parents he will be ordered to marry me. He was never happy about it at first. We barely could stand each other. Then you came. He saw you looked like him. So, he went to find work.

At first, we barely had any money to buy you the things you have now. She waits. Then you started to show signs you wanted to be with girls. I remember I was that way too. Still am. I must hide from your father. He still takes me by force. I must depend on the one I want in my life. I picture her as the one I am with. They heard him coming into the house. Let's keep this to ourselves child. Yes mama.

She goes to help her mother with the dinner. Her father looks at her. You are nearing the time to be married child. She knew not say a word. I have talked to my friend Ken. He wants you as his wife. He was my father's age. Oh god. This can't be happening to me. A man my father's age. He will be here on Saturday. I told him he can have you then. I see a look in my mother's eyes. She was shocked he would saddle her child with that brut.

They both knew he was going to bed right after dinner. He looks at his wife. I am going to sleep in the guest room. You have her things pack before Saturday. He finished eating went to take a shower. She watched her mother clinging to the table. We are both going to leave tonight child. I want you to help place the dishes in the sink. They can soak. I am going to make a call baby. Okay mama. Be careful to not make any noise. Yes, mama.

She had noticed she was calling her what she did as a baby. She went to make sure he was sound asleep. She knew he would be. She was in the pantry calling her lover. I need to get out of here and my child too. She hides her phone like always. She was washing her dishes as he came into the room. You coming to sleep with me? No, I need to get the washing done and other chores. Okay. I will be late tomorrow. He grabs her breast. You still are as hot as the first time I forced you. He was back in the room he like to sleep in lately.

He has another woman. She was nearly as young as his child. Ken wants her. That will work out. I am going to have to kick my wife out. She is getting too old for me now. When he wakes. Thinking his wife would have his breakfast ready and he could force her before he left for work. Tell her to get the hell out of his house. He would have the next woman he has been playing with.

As he goes to see if his child was at school. Found she has left the house with all her things. He goes to check on his wife. Give her hell for letting their child moved out. He had promise Ken his own child. When he went to the kitchen. He found no breakfast waiting for him. He was angry. He went to check their bedroom. all her things were gone. He sees his cheap ring on the bed.

He is running outside. Her car was gone. He has been using it while his was in the shop. Now he has nothing to get to work in. And he was to pick up Ken this morning. When he made the first call to his friend. He was finding he was banging the one he has been grooming to be his next toy to hurt. Ken said, hey buddy. Your girlfriend is a hot piece of ass. He was so angry to learn she had been playing him all this time. He reached into the box to get out his gun. Found it was gone. Dam it. He was not doing so good. Wife and child gone. His best friend stole the one he was playing with. Now his gun was gone. He smiles she could not know where I have the rest of guns at. He goes into the cellar found not one. Then goes to the attic next.

He hears a car pulling into his driveway. Found the police at his door. The door was kicked in. He was ruffly held. Cuffs were on him and even had leg irons too. He was taken out of the house. They have his keys. When he shows up at the station, He was shocked to see his friend Ken already in a cell. The young woman he has been grooming as his next wife was at her desk writing a report. She is their type. She was not looking at him. She was sent to be the target. She looks older than he thought. She knew how to dress the part. She has a lot of gray in her hair. Dam it. How was he fooled so easy. She was in her office. He sees she was the dam Chief of all things. He could not believe he was that blind. But he never did wear his glasses. Trying to look younger. He never worn his wedding ring.

Ken was not happy either. He had been played as well. Knowing the Chief of police had charmed both. They were online where men would troll for young women to play on the side with. Mostly married men. Ken wasn't. He had learned about it from his friend. She never let either of them touch her. She was a supersize woman. Who could make it seem she had barely anything. She used to be an actress before going into law enforcement. She earned her rank.

But at times she was the one to hook the men into thinking she was much younger. They had only seen a photo of her in her false looks. They had both fallen for her. Then see more coming into the station. Even their boss was hooked into the trap. She was too busy. Hooking more into her trap. She was going to be retired soon. She was going out with a high count of men falling for the same one. She was out the door to meet another. Her team were with her. She changed in the room she used. The team were in the adjoining room waiting. For the next one. This time it was one of her own. She was shocked when he had responded to her message. He could not stop what was happening to him. He had said, so much to her on the cell phone with all his text.

She had tried to tell him he should rethink about meeting her. But he said, he has wanted to see her in person. There he was being booked. The officers watch as he was being booked by the Chief. The women were more shocked he was found out. He had a bad habit. He liked them much younger. He was also married. There went his service to the police station and his pension. The Chief held a top secret about herself. She felt it was too important to withhold. She was retiring and she has only a few hours to go. She tells the Deputy Chief you will be taking my job. I have made sure of it. The woman looks at her friend. Asked you to leave to be with. She stopped, as the officers were bringing her gifts.

They were telling her she sure made her last day a full day of several arrest. She was told no one will match your arrest record. She was hugged. She looks at the place she has worked 36 years. She was going to miss some more. Her dear friend who knows her secret. Was going to be the Chief. She was going to meet her lady she has loved and taken to her bed for years. When she told her what her cruel husband had planned for her only child, she had decided the chain of arrest. She set it all in motion. To find one of her own was part of it was disappointing.

He was due to take the Deputy Chief job. But arranged for another woman instead. That had shown she was a loyal friend. She hopes the two would find their own way to see each other. She knew her lady was safe out of state. And her child was safe with her own lady a bit older. She pulls out in her personal car. She was already packed. She has her things in her car. She was on the highway heading to her love of her life. She was watching for her to come to the RV Park that has their motorhome. She had bought it two weeks before. And she has the rent paid up for 1 year. The child of her lady was not that far from them.

She sees her pulling into the driveway of their space. She goes inside. She shuts the door. And made sure it was locked she noticed the windows were closed. She was kissing her full-time girlfriend she has love so long. They would be going to get married the next day.

Leadership Comes To An End

A one-star General now. She was ready to retire. And just be her true self. She was looking at her calendar again. Yep, she was on her last day. She had served the Navy so long. She was ready to be on solid land and not being out in the ocean. She has a girlfriend she wants to have her holding her. Not letting her go. She is so stud. She was wanting her touches. Just a few more hours. She was on the deck of a ship she has become tired of being on. She gave her all to the Navy. Her love life on holds every time she had to travel overseas on this dam ship. She loved being in the Navy. She made it 36 years. She was asked to sign the papers to reenlist. But she told them I need to retired Sir. It's time I want to have something different for what's left of my life. He had nodded. He was younger than she was. And he was two ranks higher. He did not give up as many years as she has.

Her hair was jet black when she first joined. Now it's nearly white. She was a skilled officer. But. There must be something besides the Navy. She was first of the ship. She salutes the ship. And walks down the plank for the last time. She is picked up and driven to the parking lot where her car parks when she is away on board the ship, she opens her trunk. Her things are placed inside. She shuts it, she returns the salute to the Captain who drove her. The woman returns to the base. She watched the ship is pulling back out. She drives off the base. She is on the freeway. She was driving to her house. Her girlfriend was waiting for her. She was so excited to know she was coming home to stay.

She was out the door and watched the smile on her face. She runs to her. They walk inside. Just holding hands. They were now going to get back to having a real life. Without the Navy always there having her leaving on another trip. She has her battle wounds. But she is doing better with her girlfriend holding her to her. They were kissing and they were still doing it on the couch hours later. It felt good to see her in her arms. It will take time to get used to being a civilian. But they were now free to be their self. Even if it was not possible to show her true self.

They travel to get married. They were having a good time just being themselves. She had to go to the veterans hospital at times. Her girlfriend had to go to her own doctors. They could not be accepted as married. When her pension finally came, they bought a RV to live in. She wanted to see the states if they could. She sold her home. They had to stop when her wife was so sick. She was not going to make it she was informed. She sat beside her in the hospital. She was there when she takes her last breath.

She will never go looking for another woman to love. She sits watching the world go by. She decided to sell her motorhome lives her last days in the town she had buried her wife, She was place by her. She dies in her sleep. She was buried next to her love of her life. Given the 21-gun salute at her burial. No one came. But she was owned the 21-gun salute for her service she gave to the Navy.

No Way She Is The One I Remember

Joe are you ready to go to the airport? Yes, I am. Boy I sure hope I can remember what she looks like she was thinking. She was remembering a younger woman. Not one nearly 70. She was 76 herself. She has also changed over the years. Her Angel was going to pick her up. One of her own ex-girlfriend was taking her to the airport. Joe was so nervous. She had been looking for her a long time. She was trying to figure out how she might look. There stood a woman she thinks is her. Then she sees a sign. Hi, Joe it's Angel. She knew here Joe when she came off the plane. She was blushing a lot. There she was. Not certain. She limps a little. But so, did she. She was a little heavier. But so was she. Saw a woman around her age watching them. Has a lot of gray in her hair.

Angel kissed her fully on her lips. Yes, those were the thin lips she remembers. She was sure busty. Even more than she had been. Life had not been kind to her. the woman that was waiting to take her luggage was not pleased clearly to see she was not white. Never knowing her ex had dated black women. She has an annoyed look on her face. She did not like the fuss she was making over the woman. Joe was more understanding. Angle was talking to her. Joe was feeling excited to hear she has a travel trailer at lease. She was telling her it's not much to look at and she told her she isn't a great housekeeper.

When they were left off at the place. And she had paid the fare. They were inside her travel trailer. She was right about her messy place. She was being kissed so much she was holding her close. Said, you are so aggressive Angel yes, my dear Joe. Now come on let's get you undress dear. Not thinking. She is being undressed quickly. Angel was too. Joe was sucking her nipples. Yes, it's her Angel. She was making the sounds she used to. Just longer now. Joe had not been with any woman for so long. Joe needed help Angel could see. When she was told to lay down, she does.

Angel. What are you going to do to me? What you will allow me Joe. She was waking up her hungry body. She thought was dead. She was reacting to her gentleness to her now needy body. She was a great lover to her body. Angel asked her. Are you still virgin Joe. She can only nod yes. I will be incredibly careful. Remember it's a slight pinch of pain and it gone. Okay, whispers Joe. She had not thought she would want her this way. But she was waking up it seems for the first time to having a skilled woman taking her body where it never had been.

Angel asked her to move in with her and not be in that rest home. By this time, she was wanting to be with her and not stuck back inside a place she never wanted to go back to. She told her niece to help her move. She had extraordinarily little to her name. she does against her sister's wishes. She has her social security sent to the money her now girlfriend has in town. She was finding it so exciting to be able to be back in her long-ago shared girlfriend back. Her ex-girlfriend was not pleased to see the older woman living with her ex-girlfriend.

They were making her travel trailer to work for two women. She was watching as she was in another world when she was writing. But she was back to cooking. But her girlfriend was a far better cook. She had no trouble dealing with her own clutter. She did notice how she could get along with her neighbors. She did have her own health issues. She manages them. She was going to the same place as she did for her doctors.

Designing Way

We now will show our appreciation to our boss. The woman comes into the room. She was now retired, and she was given a small party for her leadership in the garment industry. She had design so many items over the 25 years she has worked for the company. Her girlfriend was standing by her side. She tells the younger women you will be the ones who will bring new ideas to this company I have given half my life to. Now you take it to the future.

Thank you, girls, for working with me to make the company what it is meant to be. Our foundation started with a small store. Now we have several stores around the world. May it grow. She was walking out the building. Not going to look back. She was forced to retire. The new owners wanted the older women to leave. Her girlfriend was another forced to retire. The new owners will learn the two they forced to retire were the backbone to the company. They were taking all their designs. The owners found out quickly their mistake.

They were told the designs were long ago copied righted to the two women. They knew the new owners had no knowledge about the business. They lost all their stores to an unknown buyer. Diane was the business. When she was forced to retire. She went to a certain skilled well know lawyer to buy the failing stores. She was not going to have the business die just because they made it impossible to work for men who wanted the business that was making good money. Staff were going to a new company. They were back with their boss. She was greeting each as they come to see her to be working with the two skilled women who were teaching the ends and outs of the business.

They changed the name. The customers that had stopped shopping at that failing business were getting the flyers from the new business. The men ran it down to the ground. They were trying to find where the money was that was supposed to be in the place. They never would find any. It was never left in the building. When they try to date the women, who work at the one where they had made true talents leave. They were pushing the women to tell them where the money is. They were told. There has never been money in the place.

The men were finding all the women were not returning to work. The men were being arrested for sexual harassment. And demanding to know where the hidden money was. Other charges were pending.

After more researching the men. Found they would target companies with woman only. Buy the company as low as possible. Try to convince the younger good-looking women to go to bed with them. Then would be taken by force to do whatever the men wanted them to do. After the women would give into their demands. But they were finding many women companies would have their staff leave at the first time they were being asked to go to bed with them.

Only one woman made that mistake. She was saved quickly. She was made drunk when she had seen them at a place, she like going. Her drink was spiked. She was lucky to be alive. All the men had been planning to take her in the alley. When men came running to stop the gang rape attempt. Now the men were in prison. She was being looked after by a doctor friend. She was soon being taken slowly and she was told you tell me to stop anytime. She was so reactive to her touches. She has had a bad crush on her doctor friend. To have her getting taken by her was a dream come true. She was not working any longer. Lives with her heart crush. Now she was being extra careful where she would go.

Treat The Problem

June is wanting to find a way to find a good woman to love. But still she has not had any luck. Out one day at a club she has not been before. Going to the bar asked for a root bear. She pays for it. Walks around checking out the ladies. Nearly all look too young but one. She has younger females staying close to her. She was still looking at the older woman. When she gets up and walks to her. The younger women were shy. She had brought them in hopes they would find someone they like. She was lifting the woman that has been watching her. She tells her young go find your birth mama girls. They were finding themselves being taken to the dance floor. They were dancing with other females around their age. Soon their shyness went away. They were having fun.

Their mama alpha takes her prize to the waiting motorhome. Glad you came in. My ex-mate can be watching our young. I wanted you if you will allow it. She was pressed up on the hall wall. She was moaning as she was taken all night. She knew when her ex-mate found the young and has taken them with her. She has her own motorhome now. When they go to a club they be in different places.

Not talking to each other. Her focus now was on her Josie. She was loving the full attention from her woman. She could not believe she was getting this lucky. To be in a woman's bed being taken so wonderfully.

She was so into her attention to know anything right then but her. Her ex-girlfriend went inside to see if she was ready to go. Thinking she would not be lucky. She was hoping anyway. She has been at her own home. Setting up something to get her wanting to have her take her body and make her want her. She was not finding her in the club. She drove back to where I live to see if she might be walking home.

I am so happy in my Polly's arms. I was marked by her several hours ago. Soon I am turning into a werewolf. I am so happy to have a hot female as my girl. We were both pregnant. Months later we have our pups. We were looking at them I was not surprised we had smaller pups. It runs in my family. I was the only one normal size in my family. She was happy. But what will her family think.

They wanted to go to see her mate's mamas. They have their young in their stroller. They were pulling onto the packs ranch. They hear a motorhome driving up to the alpha house. Her mama alpha was out the door. She waits to see who it was. Out came her middle child. She sees she has a mate too. She was a gorgeous female. She was without a mate. With the power of her beauty has the alpha wanting. Her middle child was not please seeing her alpha mama wanting her mate. She tells her mate to return to the motorhome very slowly. She was inside. Then her mate was back inside. The motorhome starts and they leave. The alpha was upset to see her middle child was leaving to keep her mate safe. That will be the last time she will see her.

This alpha has done the same with her other young but found she was not going to be able to take mates. Of course, her middle child has the one she really wanted a lot faster. She was the first to get mated to a total beauty she was trying to get closer to. The others had seen her attempt with the third sister. She barely been there a few minutes and she have her mate back in their motorhome. The other young saw their alpha try it with their own mates. She has no mate. And she hasn't tried after losing her mate to a hunter's bullet.

The Alpha Needs Her Own Mate

After trying to take her own young mates the elders ordered her to go find a mate of her own. Or else. She was gone quickly and out on her own. She was totally shy around other females. She caught the eyes of an older lesbian stud. She was the one being picked by her new friend. when the shy alpha Kio is pulling into her space she will have as her spot for the few months. Not thinking she be so lucky to have a mate so fast.

Anna has smelled a new female. But she takes her mamas with her and their mates. Anna notices her neighbor was kissing her. Anna sees a look of challenge from the woman. But she aware of her presents. Wanting to protect her soon to be mate. The alpha must calm down. But Anna grins. Hello my dear. Your human is wanting you and not willing to share you. You know who clearly, I am. How long do you plan to stay? I paid for a few months High Goddess. Not thinking I would find my mate the same day. How wonderful. I will make sure you have protection alpha female. Thank you, High Goddess.

Turning to her clearly already overprotective mate. She was known as a calm woman. And she will not lay down the law to her. Anna's birth mama comes to the woman whispering. My dear for your protection I must tell you your soon to be mate already knows. My oldest is the High Goddess. She rules this place and the town. Please curb yourself around her. She will not take her from you. You are nearing your change. So, I am going to guide into your new role. She might be alpha of her pack. But you are more dominant than she is.

She tries to calm herself. She was finding she must go into her place to turn on the calming music to calm herself. May I go to my mate now. Anna was concern now. Mama. was I wrong again. no child. She is a high wired female. If needed, we can have Sandy give her something. Okay mama. Let's see how it goes. Yes mama. Her mate was taking her to bed. Making her feel her love. She was calmed by having her mate taking her so much she forgot why she was so protective to want to guard her from the High Goddess. Anna was tossing and turning. Trying to understand what happen to make the woman so protective of her mate. To start right away. Then Anna understood why. She wants that female. And the female knew it.

And she wasn't turned yet.

Mama are you awake. I am now baby. It's clear to me why she was so protective of her mate before even turning. She saw I wanted her for my own. Oh, god baby doesn't do it I beg you child. I need Randy to help me to not go and steal her. Is it that bad child. Yes, I am wanting her so bad. Baby you get your ass over here now. Tell Bumba, you need to stay with me. No more than that. Yes mama. Bumba was watching her Anna. Female. She turns the light on by their bed.

Yes, Bumba. You were telling your mama about your need for the alpha. Yes, my Bumba. On your belly female. She does. Raise your ass. She does. She spanked her hard. She has tears in her eyes. But knows why she just did it. Now do you have the female on your mind she nods. Anna was being spanked harder. Anna was trying not cry. But Bumba was her mate. She told her the first day. It would happen. Again, she was asked. Do you still want her. No Bumba. She was spanked again. Anna's ass was smarting from her slaps to her ass. Soon she licking her hands prints from her ass. Making Anna crazy with her asshole being fucked.

When Anna did not come. She reached out to Anna. Oh, God yes do my asshole good Bumba. Baby, what is going on? Bumba spanked my ass and then licked it. Yes, Bumba faster. Oh, yes, my mate. Mama I am not interested in alpha female. Bumba made sure where my focus is supposed to be. Well good. Night baby. Anna was walking funny after beautiful Bumba worked her asshole for hours. Anna was being good around both females. They noticed Anna's mate with her, was remarkably close to her. She seems to be very calm with her there. Bumba was holding her Anna's hand. Playing with her palm with her finger. Keeping her focus on her. It was helping in the right way of keeping her focus.

Having a mate like Bumba was exciting. She keeps her Anna always focus where she needs it. Bumba loves her Anna. She will use all she can to make sure where her love is focus. Anna was pregnant so quickly. She had just weaned her last litter. Bumba was carrying Anna's young. They seem to have a strong need for each other.

Tone Down Your Actions

She is a free spirit. Always someone telling her to not act so crazy. I am not crazy. I am really doing audio books. She practices her voices. So, what if it's in public. Nothing wrong with practicing your craft. She has a need to improve what she must. She writes what she likes to write. Toning down her need to improve the make a love scene. She will keep doing her thing. She a need to create in whatever she can do. Not going to stop doing what other want her to reform doing. She is not on drugs. Her creative soul is shouting out loud to get the right attention. She keeps devoting her time to her goals. She must make it clear one way or another.

That was how it was back in the day. The virus has people wanting something different to make it through their own lives. She tries to be the one to fill the part. She is even more wanting to help with her silly ways. One is following her around. Was to see if she is in insane. She was soon giggling as she is dictating an audiobook, she was so close to her but hiding. She is recording the story. Sends it to her boss. She calls her. I was laughing like you were. She is a storyteller. Not insane.

She was back guarding this exciting woman. Oh, god she is getting on this one. She comes from the trees. Smiling at her. Hello my shadow. Have a seat. She does. She was as she looks at her changed her. Watching her reaction as she talks in one of her voices. She has her blushing as she starts the part of a book was working on. She was so wrapped in the story. She did see others sitting down to listen to her doing her audio book with all kinds of characters. She had notice they were back to listen to her. She winks at her fans. She whispers. They don't think I am insane.

She was falling hard for this woman with so many talents. No one knows is trying to make a difference. But for some reason still struggling in her life. A car pulls up in the parking lot. She sees it. She stuffs her phone into her pocket. See you later shadow. It just dawns on her she knew she was being followed. She now sees why she ran off. Her fans told the woman. You leave her alone. She is funny. She had told stories the way she wants too. This was a woman not to be stopped. But, said, I am not here to harm her. She was being brought back to the woman. She was kicking the two and said, it is not against the law to tell stories with different voices.

Please put her down. She sure can run Goddess. The woman stands there watching the Goddess. You are real she whispers. Yes, my dear. Your protector was making sure you were okay. If you can't see the love in her eyes.

She turns to see it was true. She goes to her. Gives her a firm kiss to test if she was. The way she was moaning and touching her. Said, she was ready after the story had been dictating. I see what you mean my dear. You will please allow me to listen. Blushing from her direct look as a woman would to another woman into women. She must clear her head. This Goddess was sure making her want her too. She could tell how she was affecting her. She was grinning. Her baby was sure wanting to take her that was clear.

She whispers baby you sit as close as you dare. Wait until she is telling the story. She watches the women go when asked too. They wanted to hear her voices. Now surrounded. She tells a story so racy that she was even reacting to it. As she did her voices. Was feeling her new friend she just kissed. Touching her. she was feeling the Goddess touching her too. She was doing a loved scene. She was making the sounds now that a woman makes, she was being taken. It has both females making her hotter as they did. She keeps talking making the voices and she was making the right sounds needed. She soon dropped her phone. It was picked up and the recording was stopped. She was now the one making more sounds. She was bucking as her pussy was being taken in the park. She could not help moaning so loud. The little sounds she did as she climax was not quiet.

She was so worn out after the two finally let her up. They had been warned men were heading in their direction. She was helped to get her panties and pants back on. Then was rushed to the limo. The security was making sure they were inside the limo. They rushed to their motorcycles. Following behind and in front. When the men reached the location. That hot sound of a woman being taken good, was nowhere around.

She was being taken even more in the limo. She was finding she was going with them. They go by her place. She is helped. With her younger playmate. Thank you my dear I so enjoyed you. I will return to take you to the safe room. She said, thank you G. she grins. My pleasure my dear. Baby here is her phone. She was given her phone. She said, you will need these my dear. They were her keys.

She was going inside with the younger one right behind her. She told move inside hot mama. I want more. She was doing it. The guards stay in the driveway protecting her. With someone wanting her found crazy so they can gain her money from her book sales. It was not how she received her payments. They went into a bank. Not to her home. She has other money going that way too.

Don't Lose Her

You are to bring her to me. Don't you touch her. I have someone wanting her now. Oh, really? Yes. She is coming for her. You just giving her up like that. If I don't, you will be in prison and I will be too. oh, come on sir. We should get some fun first. She is old she probably be happy we spent time with her. I said no.

He did not give a dam. She was crying when he was trying to get to her. She was where he can't reach her at all. Come on let me have you bitch. No. I don't want you or any man. She sees her lover was behind him. Closed her eyes then opens them. She closed her eyes tight. The female turned into cave lioness attacked him. His cry of horror being attacked by an animal that is not supposed to be alive. She draws him out of the building. Takes him to the river. Leaves him where other animals will eat him alive. The other man saw her. come woman. Time you were taken from here before she comes to kill you. She stays where she was with her eyes tightly shut. Not saying a thing. The man did not hear the cave lioness coming behind him. Until he feels her grabbing his head with big mouth was over his head.

He was dragged to the same place. The other animals backed away until she leaves him to eat as well. When they understood she was not returning they fought over the body. The screams of pain were heard for miles. The female returns after cleaning herself good of the scent of both men. She was wearing a luxury gown. Has another for her human she loves. She tells her softly. Come my love. I have dealt with him. She opens her eyes to see her African beauty who was the one to show her, she was desired by her. Lona was visiting South Africa and she was watching the beautiful woman come to her. Her soft lips have set her body on fire.

She was from American. She wanted to understand the location she sometimes would write about in many books. She had been caught as she was taking trip from a visitor village. She had found herself in a place she did not want to be. She had a lovely woman. She was so dark. She was beautiful. She could only think about their first touches. Then she was finding herself in a place she did not want to be. Her African beauty had found her and saves her.

She was soon laying on her bed. Being taken all night. She must keep quiet she was told. She must help her and herself back the America. She was born in the village. But she had no family any longer she wants to be with her lover. Her white skin excites her as she is touching her again. seeing her dark hand on her body has her wanting to be hers always. She will do what is necessary to get that done. she is in love with the woman. She reached out to friend who lives in America. Curon was on her way. She has documents to show this cave lioness was from America. Curon has requested Anna to go with her. instead of Katherine. She was angry with the female. They had gotten back. But Katherine not letting her know she was seeing another African beauty that worked at her largest factory. She was of noble blood. But like working. She was so attracted to Katherine. Katherine is unaware Curon is traveling to South Africa. Not far from her largest factory was located.

Anna went to see Katherine. She was not aware she was in Africa. She was so shocked to see her landing by her factory. She goes to greet her. High Goddess I am surprised to see you. Would you like to see my factory? I love too. I don't have a love of time. I am helping Curon. She a good friend needing our help. So, I will have to keep it short. Okay. She watched how the set up was and that several women were working there. It was clean and safety was considered. She was proud of how Katherine it arranged with the comfort for all the women. Even a day care. Anna was soon off and back to where she was needed. She waits as Curon helps two women get to the plane. One white and one a dark beauty. They are gone just in time. Anna was gone from the African air.

Kura

I am not letting you go without me Lora. Lora tells Kura. I was hoping you would say that. I can't leave you in here. Opening the hole wider. Being in this freezing weather. Siberia has been where she has stayed. Brought her in when she had come off the plane. Kura was soon imprisoned there. She had no idea why. At first, they ignored each other. When it became so cold Lora was shaking a lot. Kura came to warm her up. They learned each other's language.

Lora learned slower. Kura was patient with her. They would know when the guard would come with their food and water.

Little Big Mama Searches For A Hot Trucker Mama

Well, this little big mama wished she could find herself a hot trucker. She drives her pickup to a truck stop. Goes into a restaurant to check out for any. Sees several hot women she doubts are truckers. One strong woman comes up to her. She was kissed firmly. Oh, baby you do have a hot kiss. She was lifted so gentle. I would like you to be with me little big mama. She was feeling her powerful arms she was laying her head on her right shoulder. She was being held as she carries her to the table. There was a chair already for her girl to sit on. She was grinning at her new friend. She was talking to the rest. As loud as they were. Laughing along with them. She was having a great time. She was noticing they were getting their food to go. She was helped down she was walking with her new friend. You have transportation. Yes, I do. I have a little person equipped pickup. I will walk you to your pickup she was staying with her as she was walking. I want to see you more my dear. I like you so much. I like to have you as my girl. She looks up at her. She was smiling. I be honored. She watched as she was climbing into her pickup. She was nearly as high now in her driver seat. She was given a firm kiss. It has her wanting her to handle her need she has caused her. Asked where you live. She gives her the address. Sees a big smile on her new friend Tig's face. I live just down the street from you. Cate was grinning really. Yes. She wrote her address. They kissed. I need to get my loads done. I will call you when I am home tonight. She waves runs to her rig. Was gone. The rest had just left.

She goes to the store to buy food and other necessary items. One of her friend's meets her there. They go shopping at the same time. She is always helping to get the things too high to reach. They were good friends. She told her friend Cleo. I have a new lady in my life. She is normal size. Asked me to be her girl. She lives a block away. How wonderful. She will be calling me tonight. They talked about a lot of things. Always catching up. She follows her back to her place. Helps carry her things inside for her. Saves her time. She helps put her things away. Still talking away when the ex-girlfriend came into her driveway but parks in front of her motorhome.

She sees her straight friend was there helping with her groceries. They were laughing as she tries to walk inside her motorhome. But finds her straight friend blocking her way like always. I like to see Cate. She has told you no each time. Why you fall for her yourself. She grins at the ex. If I, had I sure as hell would not tell you. But no, I have not. But I could easy if she ever asked me. That has the ex-girlfriend mad as hell. You would not dare turn to women. Why not. I can catch a woman's eye easy enough. Another friend came by. Hi dear. Linda steps in front of the ex-girlfriend to Cate kissed their shared friend. She was giggling now. See what I mean. The ex-girlfriend finally leaves. The older woman said, sorry but it worked did it not. Cate kissed her too. She was fanning herself. Wow. Does that happen to you two a lot? We are not that lucky. She was blushing a lot. Two lesbians that are my friends kissed me. I cannot say I have never been kissed by lesbians now. They all were laughing. Oh my. My boyfriend is calling. They watched their straight friend leave. She runs back. Kissed both was running back to her car. They were shocked by her action.

Soon they were talking about her encounter at the truck stop. They were still talking later that night. They had dinner together. They were relaxing enjoying the star filled night. Cate was so happy to see her Tig pulling into her driveway. Her friend was going to leave so she can be with new friend. Another stronger woman gets out of car on the driver side. Walk to her. Hey honey. She turns around to see a dream looking at her. Me? Yes, you honey. She turns the rest of the way. She walks to her. Yes, young lady. She was given a kiss that has her clinging onto her as she was taken back to her place. She goes to get her car. Tig watched Kina go after the older woman. She clearly likes what she is doing. She was sitting with Cate. She was loving her full attention. Tig lifts her up heads to Cate's bed. She made her longer body work in her smaller bed. Making her, hers was so important to both.

Tig was walking to her own place with Cate laying her head on Tig's powerful right shoulder. Tig was smiling as they go into her motorhome. Her friend lived next door. She hears her coming back with her now mate. Walking so close to whisper things to each other. She was quickly undressing as Cate was. Tig rushed around shutting windows, door, and vents. Curtains were always kept closed. She lifts her Cate in her arms. Watched as she was rubbing her powerful arms. Her soft blue eyes were looking at her deep brown eyes. Cate was whispering to Tig. You are my first werewolf or shifter for that matter. Good she was grinning. I will be careful how many I give you, my Cate. She was blushing. Young? Yes, my sexy mate she has never had any. Never wanting to lay with a man ever. Many wanted the smaller beauty over the years. Her friend was so protective of her. Neither acted on their desire for each other. It was a month ago they nearly did.

They both stopped short of it ever happening. Now both have mated by their own female. Friends with friends as their mates. Anna was noting the werewolf females she has worked with while driving in their rigs were settle down finally. Both had picked best friends as their mate. Anna likes the two now mated. She was telling her mama. Two more to the ranks of shifters mama. Who? Cate with Tig. Kino with Linda. About time they were. I like Linda and Cate very much. They were walking back to get a few things. When they see a police car in Linda's driveway. Tig calls Ana. Telling her there was a policeman at Lind's. she was rushing to her place. Ana had told Kino you take her to your place. Yes Ana. Ana pulls behind the Officer. He has popped her door open. He feels someone behind him. He has burglar tools with him. She was pressing him to the police car. Ben was running to help Ana. Why did you break into her place bastard? By his ear. Orders. Ben had an alert about a fake police officer.

He was using tools to break into her travel. Hoping she be there. Take her as he has wanted. Not knowing a real police Chief would catch him in the act to break into her travel trailer. He had a boner thinking he be being forcing her. But found he was now under arrest instead. Ana has the man wanting to tell her why he was ordered here. She knew he has already lied once to her. He sees a large man looking at him. Answer son-of-a-bitch. Okay, I wanted her for my plaything. Your plaything. He was shocked when she kneed him. He was crying from the total shock and pain cause by a Chief of police. He sees the large man smile. You did not like what she did I see. How did you think the woman you wanted would react to your forcing of her body. I did not care. Ana kneed him again. The loud cry of pain was heard by many. So how do you feel about what I am doing to you bastard. I cannot take it. Did you think she would have liked it. He said, I did not care if she did or not. He was regretting his words. When she knees him even more. By then other officers were there. He was in so much pain then. Ana growls so low. Get this bastard picture. She has stepped away. Ben was holding him tightly. Stand straight bastard. He does his best. His mates the photos quickly. Ana returns. You keep him in the holding for now. No medical for him. My baby will handle him when she returns. Yes ma'am.

The fake policeman saw the woman who told him to rob her and have fun with her. A team of women pulled into her driveway. Somewhere taking the door completely off. When the criminals saw that, they were trying to investigate her travel trailer. All they see is a packed place with lots can goods only. They soon leave. One of the females was grinning that went well. Rusty oversaw the work and the officers assigned to the duty to protect her place. They knew the woman that owned it. They have flirted with her over the years. Even had her in their bed. Now she was a mated female. Made her even more desirable to have too. She walks back over by herself with female policewomen following her. She has a way of walking. She turns to grin at them. Kino was told about the ones she has been with in their beds. She was watching how the females were around her. She was right. They will want her, she can see. She walks past them. Follow me to our mate. They were running to keep up with Linda's first mate. Anna was pulling into her place. Ready for a long hot shower. She sees her Bumba backing her own rig next to hers.

Her mama came over. Hi baby. Okay what happen you would be here before I can get into the shower with my Bumba. I must sleep before tomorrow morning. I have an operation in the morning. Baby, please sit down. She gets to the point of her visit. Anna calls Ben. He was out of breath. Sorry male. It is okay. I am in a knot. She was laughing now. Please handle that bastard. I just got home and so did my Bumba. I have an operation in the morning Bumba will be needing to sleep. He said, as soon I can unknot from my male. She was laughing. More I have a feeling. Or more dragons. She hangs just her Bumba walks into their motorhome. She sees Ana was there. Hello mother-in-law. I am pleased to see you. But forgive me I need my mate then sleep. Ana said, girls please sit down. They did as she asked. She brings their first meal.

Ana was bringing the second when she sees an annoying neighbor come up to her. You are having a party. No, I am not. Get out of my driveway. She goes to Anna's takes their first plates back to her place. She had left the door open. But the man did not know Rocky was op and making him get out of their motorhome. He fell going out backwards. He was not happy to be caught trying to go into their motorhome. He was finding Anna cuffing him. She calls Ben. You finished. He was laughing. Yes, I am. He is sleeping well.

My mama's place now. He was out the door with only his pants and shoes. Saw the troublemaker cuffed trying to talk Anna out of arresting him. Shut up maggot. Walking into my mama's motorhome when she was bringing me mate and myself our second plate. Was woken from her necessary rest. Got it. The man said, I only walked into the top of the stairs to look inside. You were asked to come in did. He grabs the offered comment. Right, I was asked inside. Rocky was angry. She slapped his face hard. You were not. You were coming to see what you can steal from us. No, I was not. This time Ana was the one to slap him. He was seeing stars now.

He was to a waiting car. I will be following you. Yes sir. The man was learning his lies were not believed by these officers. As he is sitting in the back of the police car. He saw he was not going to the police station he thought he would go. And be back within a short time. They were still on the road. When he knew he would have been let out from the police station. He saw they were driving into the cargo plane where other cars are already waiting. They stayed in the car. Ben was beside them in his own car with another mate. His mate was able to catch up knowing where his mate would be heading. He has been in his dragon. Holding his clothes. He had returned to his human. Walking past the tower. Right to the car. Gets in. they kissed. They drive behind the police car. All the cars were being set for the flight to the outskirts on Nashville.

The male prison was not full right then. Saw all the men and males were lined up. The males did want to be near human. He was ignored all together. He was trying to talk to one who was saying boss can I move. They see why. Go ahead Matt. No one wanted him around them. He seemed off in some way. When his turn came, he was given the lethal injection. Then he was taken to the large furnace waiting for all the males but one. Matt taking out of the prison. Back to his pack. He was the decoy. Of males who were trying to over through his alpha father take the birth father as theirs. The males did not know they had the alpha pair oldest pup. He had related what the plan was to his fathers. Once all the traders were put down, he was feeling relaxed.

That was short lived. The alpha was watching his pregnant male carrying his son being taken by 4 males. He growls his warning. Then he broke neck of one lone male holding him as he was getting hot to take his mate too. He was moving fast. He is killing faster than the males could ever understand. None were an alpha. His mate was an alpha he fell in love with. That made their oldest an alpha that was stronger with his fathers as alphas. He was coming in as the males were attacking birth father. He was helping his alpha father them. They were not from the pack. They did not understand how weak they were until a younger male growl at his fathers. Go now. They did. But watch son. The males now looking at the male they had feared would kill them. He was fast with his attack. They were down and dead. Growls so loud that the males running to the alpha home.

The doctors go to find his fathers. He was beside his mate. He was bleeding from the force of his attack against him. The doctor told the alpha bring him our hospital. You are acting alpha son. Yes alpha. He was quick to selected males he trusted. They were out looking for the tracks of the males who had come to take the pack land they had not considered was run by males only. The one trying to kill the pup of the ruling alphas. Or that their oldest will take revenge quickly.

They see that more males were setting up a camp on the pack land. They have males from the pack tied up. They are not alphas. But they can small one many call mate. This male as acting alpha was not going to allow his own mates be harm. His first was untied told to follow the male who selected him. He runs to his male instead. The trespassers were surprise to see stronger males rushing them. The trespasser male thought he could attack the male leading strong males behind him. He was a powerful alpha male. The older male had seriously misjudged him. Found himself bent over with his pants down. He found out the danger of coming to an all-male pack. Setting up on their land. All the males were now prisoners. To do as they wish with them. The acting alpha calls his God Father. He was there quickly. Rushing to the two males he knew well. He was not fast enough. He sees the looks on the God and his face. It was the same in their own. The birth male had died from his attack they tried to save the pup. But was already dead. The alpha male had taken his own life. The elders see their new alpha returning with prisoners. He is told after the trespassers are taken to the Red Lady Ops Prisoner plane for males.

He went to his fathers. I will rule our pack now my fathers. He was ready. But he knew it had to happen. He hears from his God mamas. Catharina and her mate come to him. He was held close to Catharina. He forgets what happen. He will be a strong alpha for nearly 1,000 years.

The male had so many mates. That has made sure his blood line would continue way after he is no longer remembered. He was made to bring stronger males into the world. He was taken to be with his father's when he passed. He was one day from being 1,000. He had been protecting his last mate. He allows the much younger male that wanted him. He said, you killed my mate. So, I order you to kill me so I can be with him. The male was shocked this beautiful male rather die, than give himself to him.

His alpha waited to see what his son would do. He walked away. But returns. Quickly he was killed. He turns to look at his alpha father and birth father. I am leaving father. Killing the alpha was wrong. Seeing how his mate was devoted he was to him. Rather be killed so he can travel with him in the afterlife.

 You Will Never Get Away

Come here now woman. I keep walking. I don't know them. I am waiting for the light when I am being pulled over to a waiting car. Throw in the back seat. I am yelling help me someone please. Another woman heard me. She is yelling to her partner. Drop the food. A woman has been abducted. The Captain is rushing to the police car. Dropping her hot coffee. The Chief is calling for back up. Giving the details of the abduction of an older woman. Two white men. One driving the other in the back forcing her now. The driver was on the freeway quickly. Trying to get away. He yells shut her up dam it. The man in the back tries to cover her mouth. She bites his hand. He lets go. She was trying to find something to hit him with. Found an ashtray. Hits him several times with the ashtray. It hits his right eye. She then knees him in his balls. She was fighting for her life now.

The driver was trying to help but he was fighting the car to stay in the lane. He has a flat from a policewomen shooting at his tires. There goes another tire. The car spins out of control. The man in back was flying over the back seat and through the windshield. When the driver tried to brake. the one man was run over by a rig. That could not stop in time. The car finally stopped. He was knocked out. The woman was doing okay. But crying when she was picked up by the police Chief. It's okay. You are safe. I have you now. She kissed the Chief. Thank God you were the one. My date from last night. The Captain smiles at her mama. Hi baby. My date from last night. Chief may I know how it happened. Smiling I um was out at a club. Your mama made a bee line for me. She kissed me I was mush after that kiss. She led me to my car. She drove me to a motel. Paid for our room. We had fun. Okay Captain. Yes, Chief.

They see other cars coming. The Chief goes to them. About time you showed up. Sorry Chief. Loretta, you seem safe. Thanks to my Chief and the Captain who is my child. Captain hi. Well, where are them. One was killed by a rig. Was the one who grabbed her and tried to force her. That trucker did not have time to stop. He is over by the middle divider waiting. The second is the driver. What did you do Loretta? I bit the man who grabbed me. Fought for my life. Kneed him in his balls. And hit him with the ashtray from the back. And how was your day, dear sister. Oh, you know police work. Nothing new. What did you do after you sneak out of the club? I did notice you were gone too, Chief. I was busy with my girlfriend. Oh, really! Yes, I am holding her. I thought as much. I know you two have had eyes for each other a long time. Who paid for the room? I did sister she was under my spell. I see. The Chief was just smiling at everyone. They said, it's a good match.

My Loretta you need to go see the doctor before you go to bed with her.
Dear sister she can take me instead of the ambulance. Too late. Out
comes her big sister. You get into the ambulance now. But. No, she will
follow. Get in now. Pouting she does. Loretta is told to lay down now. She
does. Still Pouting. You stop that. I can't help it. I want my girlfriend. She
is following us. She grins. But the pain in her hand made her mad. You are
supposed to tell a patient. Sorry you don't want any. But it's the rules. If I
knew how I give you one in your hand. I am glad you don't. Loretta child
why are you here my child. Hi mama. Her girlfriend was by her side
holding her hand. Cara what happened. She was abducted by two men.
Cried out yelling for help. I was in the driver's seat hollered for the Captain
to drop everything we had to save a woman. We were on it quickly. Okay.
She fought for her life. I shot out the tires.

Her head hurts a lot. Okay baby will have you seen to. Rocky comes into
the room. She clears her throat. Females. Do we, or do we not have a
patient with a pain in her head. Giggling. Hi doctor. Rocky walks to her
patient. Loretta I will be checking you over. Female, please give me room.
Go sit down. She does. Okay tell me what. Not you Loretta. She was given
all the details. She smiles. Yep, you do want her. But X rays are necessary
right now.

You Will Never Get Away

Come here now woman. I keep walking. I don't know them. I am waiting
for the light when I am being pulled over to a waiting car. Throw in the
back seat. I am yelling help me someone please. Another woman heard
me. She is yelling to her partner. Drop the food. A woman has been
abducted. The Captain is rushing to the police car. Dropping her hot
coffee. The Chief is calling for back up. Giving the details of the abduction
of an older woman. Two white men. One driving the other in the back
forcing her now. The driver was on the freeway quickly. Trying to get
away. He yells shut her up dam it. The man in the back tries to cover her
mouth. She bites his hand. He lets go. She was trying to find something to
hit him with. Found an ashtray. Hits him several times with the ashtray. It
hits his right eye. She then knees him in his balls. She was fighting for her
life now.

The driver was trying to help but he was fighting the car to stay in the lane. He has a flat from a policewomen shooting at his tires. There goes another tire. The car spins out of control. The man in back was flying over the back seat and through the windshield. When the driver tried to brake. the one man was run over by a rig. That could not stop in time. The car finally stopped. He was knocked out. The woman was doing okay. But crying when she was picked up by the police Chief. It's okay. You are safe. I have you now. She kissed the Chief. Thank God you were the one. My date from last night. The Captain smiles at her mama. Hi baby. My date from last night. Chief may I know how it happened. Smiling I um was out at a club. Your mama made a bee line for me. She kissed me I was mush after that kiss. She led me to my car. She drove me to a motel. Paid for our room. We had fun. Okay Captain. Yes, Chief.

They see other cars coming. The Chief goes to them. About time you showed up. Sorry Chief. Loretta, you seem safe. Thanks to my Chief and the Captain who is my child. Captain hi. Well, where are them. One was killed by a rig. Was the one who grabbed her and tried to force her. That trucker did not have time to stop. He is over by the middle divider waiting. The second is the driver. What did you do Loretta? I bit the man who grabbed me. Fought for my life. Kneed him in his balls. And hit him with the ashtray from the back. And how was your day, dear sister. Oh, you know police work. Nothing new. What did you do after you sneak out of the club? I did notice you were gone too, Chief. I was busy with my girlfriend. Oh, really! Yes, I am holding her. I thought as much. I know you two have had eyes for each other a long time. Who paid for the room? I did sister she was under my spell. I see. The Chief was just smiling at everyone. They said, it's a good match.

My Loretta you need to go see the doctor before you go to bed with her. Dear sister she can take me instead of the ambulance. Too late. Out comes big sister. You get into the ambulance now. But. No, she will follow. Get in now. Pouting she does. Loretta is told to lay down now. She does. Still Pouting. You stop that. I can't help it. I 2ant my girlfriend. She is following us. She grins. But the pain in her hand made her mad. You are supposed to tell a patient. Sorry you don't want any. But it's the rules. If I knew how I give you one in your hand. I am glad you don't. Loretta child why are you here my child hi mama. Her girlfriend was by her side holding her hand. Cara what happened. She was abducted by two men. Cried out yelling for help. I was in driver's seat hollered for the Captain to everything we had to save a woman. Were on it fast. Okay. She fought for her life. I shot out the tires.

Yu-Po

You have no choice, but you can say yes and live-in luxury Yu-Po. Yu-Po makes a call to a dear friend in America. She asks to have someone translate for her. An- Li answers the translator operator. She tells the operator she will be there in 3 hours. An-Li calls in a big favor from a certain Goddess. Yu-Po hung up her hidden phone. He noticed she was still sitting where she was earlier. Well Yu-Po have you made up your mind yet. She refused to talk like before.

Looks like you will be sitting in here until you

WHAT DO YOU MEAN WOMAN

I am walking to a new club. I peeked inside. Yep, all women. I boldly strut inside. I asked for coke. Not my favorite. But bars don't sell what I liked. I am using a straw and slipping slowly. I am out of place here. But I love every single hot black woman in the place. I am sure being watched a lot. I walked right into little person. She was looking up at me. Hi, I am Bumba. I am Jo. Like to dance with me. Sure, I tell her. She was dark and she was loving how I was holding her up in my strong arms. Yes. I work out. The ladies love it. She was giggling because I was so willing to hold her close as we danced. She was holding on and I was exactly to one dancing. She was kissing me a lot. I asked her. you claiming me honey? She grins. My heart was beating a happy dance. Yes, you sexy werewolf. I growl low in her ear. She moans. Oh, I need you, Jo.

I see several females coming to me. She was lifted from me. She cries. No, I picked her first two other females were there quickly. Lifting Bumba from the other female that had removed her. Jinn-Linn was hurrying over too. she growls extremely low the other females leave. They were wanting me I see. But I am given Bumba. She licks my ear. I nip hers. She lets out a sigh. Jinn-Lin takes my arm. She was making a sexy growl now. I decided to nip her sexy ear. She does it in return. Bumba smiles nips my other ear. I am grinning. Sherry was beside me and decides I need another nip. May was back with her Sara.

Finding out I had attracted Goddesses made me feel special. I was holding my Bumba. She loves playing with my muscles. Jinn-Lin and Cherry walk around talking to friends and new ones. The one that dare touch Bumba was gone. She was extracted so quickly. It was barely noticed. There are always guards near the Goddesses. Bumba was the smallest. She was always looked after. I was soon following my 3 mates. I was riding my motorcycle. It had a side car. Bumba wanted to ride in it to be with me. So, Jinn-Lin rode behind me Sherry gets in the side card. Held Bumba close to her. With the seatbelt I had made sure was tighten enough to not hurt Bumba. They had ridden with Sara and May to the club. Now I had my three mates. they were going with me. They were enjoying being with me. I finally head home. To find my mates lived where I do. I was new to the Park. Our protector was grinning a lot. Because I am winking in my mirror.

Jinn-Lin was playing with my big breast under my leather jacket. I was growling when she was. I stopped. Turned around gave that dam tease a kiss that has her breathless and moaning. She was being so good with that kiss letting her know I was going to handle her soon as I can. She has the biggest motorhome she thought. Was trying to get me to go with her. I lift my first Bumba was giggling when I give her a kiss, she has yet had I bet. I said come see your mates motorhome. Watch out for my weights. Sherry whispers let's hurry our mate. We have company. She turns to see her mamas. They come up to me and see I am marked even if it's on my ears to start.

They were smiling at me. You don't go hunting for one new girlfriend baby. You come home with three Goddesses mates. They waited for them to be allowed to approach closer. Bumba smiles. It has both smiling at her. hello their honey. Bumba said I am her first. I am Bumba. Jinn-Lin smiles I am Jinn-Lin, and I am her Second. Looking at Sherry. I am Sherry her third. I see my sister running up to see who I am mated too. they are all little persons. Bumba was smiling at them. She said hi girls. I am your sister's 1st I am Bumba. Jinn-Lin was at their level hi girls I am Jinn-Lin your sister's second mate. Sherry was at the level too. I am Sherry your sister's third mate. They asked if Bumba could stand with them and see if she is taller. I am letting her down. She goes up to them. She is giggling. I am taller Jo.

I look at my Bumba. She said, forgive us please ladies we have plans with Jo. They are all giggling. Come for breakfast tomorrow girls. They all said thank you. I am being tugged by my mates. They go inside first. I thought I should pick Bumba up. Told her I wasn't knowing I have a beauty like you coming or I would have my step I have when my big sisters come to visit. I was the one they have depended on since I was big enough to fight their fights for them.

They see she was right she had a lot of weights all over the place. Her sisters were used to it. Soon her sisters were finding females coming to visit them. They were being courted by several. All normal size Red Lady Ops were finding them too beautiful to be without a mate as their age. They were being chased by ones their age. They have a feeling Jo's mates had a lot to do with it. Jinn-Lin had a long talk with Anna. They were playing matchmaker. So, the little females can have a family like their little sister has now. I am looking forward to having my own mates young.

A few days after Christmas I meet the one Goddess that all look to for the guidance they need. I was home by myself. I was working out. I will be leaving for the Professional Women Bodybuilder contest. I love going. I have of bunch friends who are in the same contest. I was hoping to win this year. I see a striking female. I am opening my door quickly. She smiles as she comes inside. She was seeing I was back working out. My mates will be back High Goddess. She grins at me. I am here to talk to you. Oh, I placed my weights down. Would you care for something to eat. The grin on her face did something to me. I was trying extremely hard to think about my mates. And it made a big difference. She nods. You are being incredibly good. You will be given the right to be the Goddess they have asked I do. But I will wait here until they return. I will have water thank you. I grin. I find a large glass for her water. Placed cookies out. Please forgive me. I am leaving soon with my mates to go to the contest. I understand if you like to get back to your weightlifting.

Her was going so um well. She was driving me crazy. I was so glad when my mates came home. I was working out. Went to help Bumba up. She lifts her arms up. She was kissed so much by me. She whispers I need your attention my Jo. Jinn-Lin was getting more kisses from me too. Sherry was next. She was given as many kisses as possible. My mates saw the extra-large glass of water. She was enjoying the last cookie. Saying um so good. They saw my face. I was taking Bumba to our bed. she was howling as she was enjoying my loving. Anna was trying hard to not laugh. Your poor mate was being so good around me. They grin. Was she now. Yes. She is good mate, so you don't have to worry. Oh, we like how you mess her head up. We will gain the fun with her. Jinn-Lin was pulled into their room next. Bumba was coming back in the front room. Hi Anna. She was grinning. You want more of Jo's cookies. Yes, I would. She used her ladder she was given as her birthday gift. Anna watched as Bumba was being a host while her shared mate was with another mate. She notices she was pregnant.

She gives anna her plate of cookies. She watched as she goes to open the door. Hi come in. Anna sees her mamas coming inside. They fussed over her. she was giggling when they noticed she was showing more. How many Bumba. Rocky said I am having 8 little ones like me. That is wonderful Bumba. Would you like some of Jo's cookies. Yes, thank you they said. Milk? Yes, I know we both could use some. She is getting it herself. She was acting like a true mated female. She was comfortable with her life with Jo. Well hello baby. Hello mamas. How was your day? Busy they said. Your? Oh, just taking time out.

Oh, really. Yes. Sitting here for um 3 hours. Watched Jo working out with her weights. I have been drinking this ex-large glass of water and had 2 helpings of Jo's cookies. I need to run to a toilet. Without upsetting that hot female mama. she was trying so hard to be good. She has her mates so wild in their bed. I am trying so hard to be good mama. she was whining now. Ana said come on baby. She takes her hands. Checks to be sure Jo wasn't in the bathroom. Anna was inside the bathroom. She was moaning as she was peeing a lot from dam ex-large of water. She cleans herself in the bathroom. Her mama takes her hand back to go back to the front room.

She was back in her chair. Mina was starting to laugh, and Ana was too. you know she had you take her many times outside to guard her as she use the one, we had. I know. Anna was blushing. Jo sees Anna and she had heard her in the bathroom moaning from having to hold her pee and getting to do it. Jo. Jerked her off the chair. Takes her to the bedroom she was wild eyes with shock she had done it. you female I was saying are not with a mate I see. She can only nod. And I can see your need is out of control. She nods again. She has never had an alpha female take her control from her as she was doing. She was on her back. Naked. She was being taken hard. She was reacting to her demanding way she was being. She was soon out of her high heat. But I was not done with this female. She was on her knees and I was fucking her asshole with a large dildo. That female clearly loves it done. She was kept unstable as I work her until she was safe to go out the door. I was now going to claim as my mate. She was looking at me. She just nods. I have her now. She was smiling now. Being handled by this powerfully built female. She was clinging to me more. Her mama came into the room sees she was claimed by me.

Ana was going to try for me. I can see it in her eyes. She was like her child. I was getting hooked on that female now. Ana was on my bed. She summits to me too. I only will have Goddesses in my bed. Now I have another female who is looking for her mate. I am behind her now. Mina. She turns slowly. Looking at me. She can only nod. I am carrying her inside. She sees her mate and her baby both watching as I am taking Mina to my bed. she was watching as I undress. She knows I am going to claim her too. she is undressing and comes to me. I am taking her as she bends over. She was allowing me to do this. After she well looked after she was following me. I was finding I am having a lot of females going to have my young. Bumba goes to my newest mates. She grins at them. You are to pull your motorhome closer. A space is opening. They said, yes Bumba. She was the first mate. They hug her. She growls. They giggle. Jinn-Lin was smiling how Bumba made it noticeably clear who was the first mate. It was her right to do so.

Linda came to visit one day. Not knowing Bumba was a first mate. I happen to come behind her. she was moaning from my powerful alpha scent. She turns around. I give her a hard kiss. She was moaning now. She said, you sure alpha you want a bat ear fox. I whispered I have my bat ear fox Bumba as my first mate. She was disarmed by how I was kissing her neck. You have no claim mark female. She was getting chills I could tell when I was licking her neck. She could not take it another moment. please make me yours too. she was on my bed. I have her for hours as she was taken as my mate. She was so happy to be mated by a powerful alpha. She was taking a shower when my Bumba came home next. she smells I have had her friend Linda. She was wanting me to lift her up. She said, you will need to get me to the hospital. I am getting my extra big leather jacket. Told Linda. I must rush my first to the hospital I am told we will go in my Jeep mate. I kissed her. after I kissed my Bumba. She makes a call. Get Rocky now. Bumba is coming in hot. Babies want out. Rocky takes the phone. I will be ready. I am driving my mate we share. Rocky was saying I understand Linda.

Their friendship was not as it had been. Linda now was going to be loyal to her Jo. I am an alpha who can make most Goddess want to play with. I have so many now. I was thinking I would never be attracted to more. I should have remembered. I am a magnet. When they learned I have the mamas of Anna too. they were shocked at first. But when they meet me. Different story. Tower was having a hard time I saw to not get closer to see my muscles. She was grinning. You are bigger than I am sweety. I walk around her. she was watching me as I was touching her. she was not with a female. She was whining low. She was looking at me with a certain I understood. She was taken to her place. I was on her hot body. I was licking her all over she was climaxing as I was licking her. She was so wanting by that time. She was giving me her alpha body. That has me driving her to places even Anna and Ana had not gone before. She was so sensitive to my every touch and licks. She was the first to be treated like I was. She was soon my mate. She was staying at my motorhome. Working out with me.

Rusty was trying to find Tower. She saw her working out at my place. She noticed I had her as my mate too. She made a mistake one day. Letting her guard down around me. She was soon letting me kiss her. all my mates watched how she was getting around me. My kisses were getting to demand she was undone by my first mate. She goes to her bigger friend. Asked her why not give in Rusty. My mate wants you too. she looks into my eyes. She was on my lap kissing me. It was her last mistake. I take her quickly. She was my mate so quickly. She was now under my spell for now. I will let so many go soon. So, they can have a new mates. I am a Goddess. I am holding onto my Bumba, Jinn-Lin, Sherry, Linda. I knew when my Anna and her mamas were ready to go find new mates. I had made sure Tower and Rusty were back together.

Each I had taken after my first 3 and Linda were back looking for a new playmates. I could not let them stay longer. In fact, I did it earlier than they might have left. Jinn-Lin was the one to ask. She was pleased I was so concern for them. She was with me each time I told them why I was doing it. They kissed me and moved on with their lives.

When The Wind Blows

I am out in the high winds. I was laughing as it was pushing me around. I was drunk. The woman who had kept having me drink. Who knows what happened to her. I was alone. I am drinking even more saw trash can and dropped in it. Have another and drinking it down fast. My backpack was full of more. I was being watched. I did not know I was being watched. She was wanting me. I was being knocked down by a wolf. I am smart to not look at the eye of this female. She turns her head back and forth. I am giggling as she does. She washed my face. I hugged her after she did.

She walks with me as I keep walking. I take my backpack off. She grabs it. And runs with it in her teeth. I tried to keep up with her. I lost her quickly. The werewolf turns into her human throws out the full bottles then thought. No, I think I am going to open them and empty them out. She hears her calling to her. she cuts herself and limps back to her. She was saying were you attacked for my booze. My head was spinning now. I think I need to sit dow. I did hard. The wind was no longer funny. I was throwing up.

She was turning into her human. Was lifted by a hot looking powerful woman she passed out. And she was snoring. She kissed her. The motorhome pulls up to her. Opening the door. She was helped inside as she holds her mate. Mama she was drinking a lot. I can smell it baby. She was forced at first by a woman at her own home. Where is that bitch. Took care of her mama. She will never do that again. Where did you take her backpack. She takes it out of her jacket. Her mama smiles. She said look what I put in it. She looks. She was smiling. My baby you made it clear. We will be at the hospital in about 10 minutes. My mate are you about there? She turns said, I am here now. They are coming now.

They go to the bathroom. She is being lifted by the younger female. She was now dressed. She was thinking she better or she will be attacked by the policewomen at the paranormal police station. She was a rare beauty. Many in there have been trying to get her for their selves. She worked there. Her mamas were protecting her now. If a female comes too close to their baby, the females were confronted and finds two incredibly angry mamas protecting her. Even when one female they knew can demand her to be hers. if she requested her to be her mate. But she did not want that female. She would just be just one of many. She has her own female.

But was wanting more in helping this female's future mate. She growls when several females were coming to try to claim the rare beauty as their shared mate. That was the time the human throws up again. They were running to go home. Growling their plan to have Licco was shot by that drunk woman throwing up on their clothes. They were a family of Puma cross Bobcat. They see she had thrown up blood. Doctor Rocky was at work. She tells the nurses. X rays right now. They were running to get x ray with Licco right behind. She takes over the bed. Moving even faster than the nurses could. She was at the door. She helps her to the bed for x-rays.

Rocky started growling. Looking at the beautiful female. Who was with many females. She told her about her finding at a woman's house. Being forced to drink a lot of booze. She was growling. The x ray tech. said doctor look. Was the bitch trying to kill her. Where is she. Looking right into her eyes. I killed her doctor. Good female. I want the address they heard the woman say the address. She spoke. Why would I want to drink stuff. I am not one to drink dam it. They listen., that not called for. No, I am not going to give myself to a smelly bitch. Dam it that hurts. I am getting out of here. She was acting out she was thinking. Dam it this bitch think I would be her whore.

After getting me to drink that drain-o. I am feeling a need to pee. To pee? She did a lot. Smart nurse was collecting it right then. Have Sandy look at the blood nurse. Yes, doctor. Sure hope no one is watching me as I pee by this dumper. Wow. Look at all the booze. I am already drunk. I can just use this and maybe the drain-o will be flushed out. Rocky was growling loudly. Where is the body? At the address in the large bedroom in the closet. Go get it now females. They were the ones that had their clothes dirtied by her. When they saw they were in the x ray. They were going to confront the human. Then they heard why she was so sick. Rocky looks at all of them. I will cover the cost of uniforms. They were given the address.

They rushed over to the house. Men were lining up to take the woman as they wished. The woman in the house had promise. She would be so drunk she will not know they were going to do to her. But the house was dark. They see the men standing from the house down to the next block. The woman was found when they went to the back. Found the dead body. They drag her out the front door. The men see the woman was being dragged out the front door. She was smelling ripe by now. The men were leaving in all directions. But found men surrounding them. They closed ranks. The men were finding they were heading to the large paddy wagon. The females bring the body in with the body bag.

Sandy was checking her out. She looks at the younger female. So did Rocky. Then the females were looking at her with a different look. As a skilled assassin. She had worked as one for this killed was clean. No telling how she had been killed. But the doctors can see how it was done. The anger behind it was there.

Her mamas were grinning. You sure did her good. You will be hired by that group that sent you to college. Rocky looks at her skill. You two taught her well. She will be having that job as quickly as I can arrange it. But for the moment. Her human needs to be helped. Nurse the charcoal now. Yes doctor. You female stay by her. Do not leave her. She nods. Rocky looks at her over protected mamas. You will be needed my dears your skill in her training. Has told me you will be needed as well. They nod. The females that had wanted her for so long were looking at her as a hero now. Not a shared mate.

Rocky sees their mamas coming to collect them. Rocky looks at the mamas. You bring your cubs to Timberland for training. They looked at them next. You have learned a lesson in reference to this female? Yes, she is the human's mate correct. You will be trained by her mamas. She has hers eyes on the females. I like to see you both in my office right now. Sandy, please watch her progress. Yes Doctor. If anything goes wrong, I will be right back to help with her change. I don't want to have to take her away from her female. Understood doctor.

Sandy is the one giving her the charcoal. She was trying to stop them from giving it to her. The one she was relaxed with has her looking into her eyes. She was told you keep looking at your mate's eyes female. Yes Licco. The females were not wanting to leave. They were spell bound by Licco too. She knew her mamas were in their faces. They looked down. These werewolf females were making them behave. All sudden they were going with the older females. And right into a safe room. Ordered to look at the wall don't move. They were doing it. They go out the door. Lock it now nurse.

The dyke nurse asked, can I just go in there and claim them instead. They were grinning they go back into the room. Turn around right now females. They do. You will tell this dyke nurse to take you all as her mates. They were looking at the hottest dyke in a nurse uniform that was a full Puma. They go to her. Please make us your Puma female. She said to the werewolf females. Thank you, females. They said they should be with their kind. Walked out of the room. Locked the door. Grinning. Walking back to see how things were going.

As they return to the room. They see their baby being taken by her human. She was sure taking her hotly. They were getting closer and closer to her. Wanting her attention. She grins. Please sit-down females. I want to make this hot female my first. Then she was quick. As her first was quickly off the bed. Grinning when her birth mama was the next one taken by her. She ordered her mark her now. She does and she was climaxing as she was. With the alpha female coming to this exciting human. She was tasting her mate own her lips. She was watching as her mate moves quickly the alpha female was getting taken now. She was howling in excitement. She was loving her own work out. Their baby finally knew who was the most vocal in her mamas bedroom.

Sandy came running into the room. Found the alpha mama of the younger female was being taken. Running back to the room. Rocky was watching this woman taking the alpha mama. She was sure hot as she had taken her from behind. She was using a strap on dildo. Making that older female wanting and she was wishing she would do that to her. She has two puma cross bobcats wanting her. She grins. You will be next my felines.

They were undressing and waiting as she finished making the alpha so happy. She sits with her now ex mate and their only pup. As the birth mama was next to get the work out, she has needed. She was grinning as she yowls as she was being taken. The dildos were adding up. She said I like more in here now please. The alpha puma cross bobcat went to get them.

Rocky could only watch from the window. As this woman has them all wanting her talents. The next alpha was worked harder than her now ex mate. Rocky smiles. This woman had made it so clear she will have them. Rocky had wanted them. But they had said, our true mate is in that room when they came back to the room.

Sandy was looking at her mate. She was taken to their shared room the sleep in when at work. Sandy takes Rocky as she was begging her to do. Her first come to the room. Unlocks the door. She moves Sandy. You let her take your pussy. She was moving to where Rocky could take her pussy. Rocky smells her first behind her. bend over my mate now she whispers as she licks her right ear. I am going to fuck your pretty asshole my hot mate. She was going in so easy. She was on Sandy's pussy. When she howls it's in Sandy's pussy.

The hospital was sure having lusted up females being taken. The females downstairs were peeking into the rooms. The human was back on her first female. She was enjoying her body more. Between the howling and yowling the females were so looking at the human working all the females with her hot body on display has so many howling or yowling to be allowed inside. The nurses were calling every so often. You want more Dina. She sees which was in the offering. She was grinning soon she was a remarkably busy woman.

Dina was soon turning. She had a dormant Dragon in her. Her mates watched as their sexy mate was in her full-size dragon. The room was made taller for her Dragon. They were shocked they turned into a bit smaller Dragon. There was two Dragons her size looking at their baby.

With her smaller dragon mates. She goes to the window. She purrs at her mamas. They return the purr. Rocky had done a D N A on her blood.

Found a notice about two females that have been looking for their only young. When they saw a reply. They contact the Alpha House at Timberland. Talked to Treasure. She had them follow her as she flies to the hospital. After the 3 females were at last relaxed and calm then come to where the two Dragons were watching their grown baby was being looked after. They were so proud she has so many females. Oddly, they were all dragons. Not what they once were. The Dominic gene from their true mate. Was making them into Dragons only. Rocky was so surprise when they were full dragons. She checks each female. No wonder the puma cross bobcats had been so sure she was their mate.

The next day. Following her mamas with her 30 mates flying with her. They were returning to Spain. They were living in a hidden castle. They went in first. Calling the females to come to honor their new alpha Dragon. They were lining up as Dina comes in her Dragon with her mates. They were shock seeing this one female with her 30 mates with her. Dina first was walking with her. They could see she was. She was wearing the same crown as her royal mate did. They were watching as the mates circle her. They did not need to be told how to do it.

They seem to know they were to do. Dina smiles and she heads to her chambers with all 30 following her closely. One female was not pleased to see her back and had taken her place as the Queen of all the females. She did see the assassin that came for her. The woman where the true queen was staying was the child of the female who told her own child. Make sure is given poison and you make her drink all the booze she had bought. Then have her taken by all the men and let them take her as they liked to take women. Hoping one would kill her. She had plan to steal the royal throne for herself. Her stepsister had no right to the throne that was taken by her own mama.

She was not killed in the castle. She was taken to a place far from Spain. The one that takes the responsibility was Rocky. She had requested the honor to handle it. She was granted it. She had come in her Dragon. She had been waiting for the female to show herself. She did. And she was so shocked as the one dragon she sees is the one that will end her life. She was taken by Rocky's dragon guards. She lands on the smaller female taking her by her shoulders of her dragon. She was held like a baby dragon would be.

She was not able to defend herself from the Earth-bound First Goddess. She was taken over the black seas She was torn apart. And she was soon only dragon meat for the oldest known Megalodon shark. She had called them to feed. Her young were there feeding on the big meal. The smaller male could share the meal of dragon. They will part from each other until it was time to breed. Her young will disappear before she would have time to feed on her own young.

Rocky watched how that female was looking at her with a certain. She wasn't sure it was. Rocky was gone with her guards. She had seen something oddly sexual interest. But it passes as fast as it had come. Rocky was heading home. They fly over the clouds to keep from being seen by human's. time they reached American shoreline it was dark as she glides down. To be greeted by her mate. She has her clothes. All the females even Rocky wanted to get a bath before going inside. Her mates watched all went to the dragon bath to clean all the blood and they were being washed by the dragon female that service the dragon guard only. Treasure was making sure she was the one to wash her mate herself. She was so lovely in her dragon. She was giving her dragon self to her mate. They were playing in the giant bathing pool.

They Can't Part

Regina Drives her old Mack. Finding jobs here and there. Barely making it. She was once a housewife with no man in her home. She let a man in her life once. Has a child from him. But lost her from his way of beating her in her stomach. She was nearly dead. Thank god he had left the house. Told her he be back to bury her after work. She had called an old girlfriend. Asking her to help her. She was there quickly. She had to kick down the door. He was not as he appeared at first. She was rushed to the hospital.

She was transferred to San Francisco. A good hospital that was there when a call was made by her girlfriend. She wanted her safe. They tried again to make it work as roommates. But once she was able to leave the hospital. Their relationship as friends fell apart. She knew it would. She spent years trying to get over losing her baby girl. Found jobs where she was able. Had a nice one for years. Saved all she could. Trained to be a trucker. At last, she had her CDL. She drove company rigs for many years.

One day she found a job looking after a woman on her off days. She protect her from punks. When she was gone doing her company job she was contacted by a lawyer. Ma'am I know you are driving right now. Where will you be staying this evening after you have to take your required rest. She asked, why is a lawyer contacting me sir? It's best we meet in person. Where will you be staying when you stop to rest and eat. I will meet you in the restaurant. She told him. He was considering her being a woman she would want to feel safe. She gave him about the time she will be at the truck stop. She told him what her rig and trailer said. Okay. I can be there in time. She was finished with her last load for the day. She drove to get her trailer loaded.

She was pulling into the truck stop. Saw a limousine waiting. Saw a man coming out of the limousine. The woman driver was checking her out boldly. She was walking with the man she is climbing down from her rig. Hello. I am the lawyer for Sara Daniels. She spoke highly of your kindness. I have been her lawyer after she was married. Her husband made sure I would look in on her. I know you were on the weekend. She had no children. She told me. You were as close as a child she had. She looks at him as they sit down. The woman was on her side. She looks at her a lot. But said nothing. He hands her something to read.

It was a blue document. She was shaking as she was reading the will. She was giving her all she had. Her things are being kept safe for you. A friend of my driver has agreed to wait for you to go to the place to look over what she has ready. She looks at this woman. You glow. Yes, I do. I will be the one driving you my dear. It has her feeling oddly amazingly comfortable. I am going now. She will be looking after you. She watched him leave. She was watching her getting closer. You need attention Honey. She was blushing. I have not been with anyone in so long. And never a woman. She feels her touching her thigh. Moving between her legs. She was reacting to her touches. She feels her move her hand. Hi May. Hi Shirley. May said, my regular meal. Yes. Shirley said, same as usual. Yes.

The waitress knew both. Did not know they knew each other. May said I will be riding with you honey as you handle your last loads. You will be going with me afterwards. She looks at this beautiful dark beauty looking into her hazel eyes with her brown eyes. Let's get a shower. They finished eating. They go get one shower together. Shirley was wanting to see what she wants with her in the shower. She was drawn to want her touches. She can't understand why. But she does.

They go in the shower room. May locks the door. She is helping her undress. She watched as May undressed. She was kissing her so tenderly. May. I need you to take me. I don't understand why. I will be slow so you will not feel fear. Thank you, May. You are welcome my dear. She kissed her lips with her full soft lips. So different than the only man she had when she was still young. She was hungry for more. May lifts her up. Takes her first taste. Keep your mouth covered. She found out quickly why. She was being taken only where her own hand had been. She was finding she loves it done. She climaxed harder than she thought she could.

After that workout. She was so wanting around May. Shirley was smiling when she was trying her best to return the favor. May was excited as she made her climax. Her legs were shaking from her own climax. She was washing her mouth out. Said, you tasted so sweet my dear. May tries to talk. Oh, honey you have me feeling so good too. She has her close to her. I need to tell you something before we can go on. I feel your need. I have it too. I will tell you when I feel it's right.

May needs her now. They were in her sleeper again making love together. May had told her what she was. By then she was so in love with May. She can't see herself alone after she taught her about her own body and what she is having done and doing back to her May. May had Anna pick them up in her smaller plane. It was easy to in and out of tight places. At least for Anna. She had landed by the company that Regina worked she had to return the rig and trailer. She was quitting. They told her she was the best woman driver they had. She had worked so long. She receives retirement.

She goes with her mate May. They run to the plane. She was being kissed by May. She never tired of having her full soft lips on her thin ones. She was what she never knew she has desperately needed in her life. Month later she was smiling to see she was carrying their tiger cubs. Anna was so sweet to her. all the females were. She finally looks at the things she was now the owner of. So surprised to know they had lived simply. But was rich. It was protected by her lawyer. She had made her will years before. She knew one day she would be back with her husband in heaven in her mind.

Regina learns she has dragon too. She was practicing with her beautiful May showing her. Regina has never known love like she has with her mate May. May learns if she strays, she will lose her Regina. Anna was on, May when she was spotted checking out a new female to Timberland. Anna told her after the female went to her mama's to stay. She is mated. She had come behind the tiger you ever hurt your mate by cheating you be dealing with my paddle. May never looks at another female but her loyal and loving mate. All knew the top females were in a commented relationship. They were the prefect role models.

May decides to consider moving. But she had to ask her mate. Regina has a talk with her. My mate you love me. Yes, my love. Then you will be staying here until we want this for both. Not because you were caught looking at a mated female. She shows her paddle Anna gave her. She hangs it on the bedroom wall. May was looking at her female she genuinely loves a lot. Smiling at her Regina. She now knows she is hers forever. She was after all the one who help her understand who she was after May had taken her for time. She had not been with anyone after being saved. And she carries her young. Anna was right. May takes her Regina to bed. they were still in bed the next morning.

May has the paddle framed with these words. THE PADDLE OF REMINDER WHO LOVES YOU. Not saying a word. May made dinner. Saw Regina was exhausted. She sees how May had made a big dinner. Exhaustion forgotten. She sits down as May kissed her deeply. Gave her a ring she had trouble getting the right gem in. May was on her right knee. Looking into the hazel eyes she loves. Will you be my forever mate. Let me make you a Goddess so I never lose you Regina. She finds Regina knocking her over then staying on top of her. You want me that long my Beautiful May who taught me what my body needed. Yes, I do my Regina. I have never wanted any other like I want you.

She asked, where is the paddle? She smiles. In the bedroom where it belongs. She told her I saw it gone. I was over talking to Anna. Come see for yourself. She goes not wanting to find it missing like it was. Anna comes into their home fired up and ready to use the paddle. When she hears Regina laughing. That's why it was gone. Anna leaves quickly closing the door. They call Anna. Come back here female. Bumba saw Anna leaving home. She runs to Anna swings her around. What were you doing my mate. Anna kissed her after she lifts her up walks by to May's and Reina's house. She whispers what she was going to do to May. The look of shock had her fire up too. Easy my mate. Let's see why I must return. She lets her down. Holding hands, they go inside. Anna and Bumba were shown the ring May has for Regina. Then what May did with the paddle. Anna was laughing. That's so sweet what you had written.

She is my heart and soul Anna. Now that you are here. I like you to make my mate a Goddess. She is my life mate. Anna told both I would be honored. Ana and Rocky ran to stop Anna from paddling May. They had seen what she had done. They walked inside to see Anna in front of Regina with her May nearby being made a Goddess. They both were smiling. This was more like it. Rocky was with Regina later that day. She had been doing her exam to see how soon she was going to have her May's young. She was with Bumba on first day as paranormal nurse. With her heart breaking thinking she was not going to be hers any longer. To finding a big meal waiting. A ring, And the paddle with the words in a frame.

She was given tiny kittens needing a mama. Regina turns into her tiger nurses them. They were hungry the bigger nipple was a challenge at first. But May was helping them, and they soon were sucking her tits. They grew fast on her rich tiger milk. May was smiling as the orange tabbies were following Regina around. They were only 4 weeks looked like grown cats. Goddess tiger milk was making them grow. They still meow like kittens. Sandy checks them. Smiles. All healthy Regina. Your own cubs are coming maybe today or in the morning. You might as well stay here. May smile when she sees an unasked question. I will feed them my mate. Sandy, do I have time to run home get what she needs. Yes May. First, she gives her kittens to her to nurse while she was gone. She was still nursing them.

May asked. What else my mate she makes certain sound that has May right by her side. Anna peeks in heard the sound she has not heard in so long. She watches May rush to her Regina. She licks her face. May was smiling. What a way to keep me close she was telling her mate. I am near to having our cubs darling that has May turning and waiting as they came. Bumba has the older kittens with her nursing on her. While Regina has them like any female tiger. No time to turn. She was not going to lose her girls if she can help it. She looks at Anna. Yes, after you deliver your girls that are alive Regina. They were talking through their minds. Every Goddess can now.

The cubs were smelling the kittens. They went to their mama with May's help. She takes the kittens from Bumba who of course has bonded to them after feeding the big kittens. She looks at her mate. Anna grins at her. Yes, my mate. I will see what I can do. But let's get puppies that has Bumba running to her and bounced on Anna. She is falling her mama was there quickly. Anna was giggling. My birth mama always ready to save me. Bumba was giggling. Rocky ran and stopped her from falling. Mama-in-law saves my mate. Rocky was giggling now. Ana was there.

At last, the last tiger cub was being washed by their alpha mama. The kittens found a place to nurse too. It was good they were. Means they would be always protected by their younger sisters. They thought of May and Regina as their mamas. They grow into bigger cats the smallest of the tiger cubs Little May asked her mamas if she can mate her adopted sisters. They all were females. She wanted them over another tiger female. She was so happy when Little May goes to them to see what their mamas said. They said yes. Because they had grown up to be part shifter from nursing their mamas milk, they were able to talk and like any shifter could turn into a human. With a little help from their mamas only they had that ability. They were mated to little May. She was a good alpha mate to all of them. Knew if her smallest cub could be loyal. She could try to be good for the sake of Regina she will try to get her life stable she watch how she was acting all the time.

May was talking to a friend one day. She had hugged her. May walks up to her. Placed her in her hand. Walks away. Not saying a word.

Bob Cat Driver Takes Job As A Trucker

Paula was tired of driving a Bob Cat. She would drive on the weekends. Made more in two days than a month as a Bob Cat Driver. She takes off for a month and drove for the same company who had her driving weekends. She was shocked how much more she has made in a months' time. She quits the first job. She was driving long hours making good money. She quick on doing her log. Keeps up on rig payments. Had it paid and soon was getting her trailer. She loves the perks that came with the job. Her meals are covered her fuel, even repairs. She loves the long hot showers in the truck stops. She has her motel room covered. She loves that too. She like having time off as much. She was going out to clubs she found.

She met one gal that has her wanting her with her. She goes to see her. her ex-girlfriend shows up. When her Diane saw her pulling up in rig. She tells her move out of the way. The woman did not like her around another. But she did move out of the way as Paula back her rig in the driveway. She gets out. Paula was well built. Strong arms and extra-large breast like Diane has. When Paula came up to her Diane, she told the ex-girlfriend to get lost. They go to her rig. Paula helps Diane into her rig. What do you want from your trailer. She has two tiny yorkies. She finds her jacket. She went to her compartment under her seat. Placed heavy duty paddle locks on both doors, she had bought. Was told they could not but be cut as easy. She lifts the dogs. They licked her face. Saw the ex-girlfriend. They were growling at her. She backed away from them.

Walking to the other side. Gives her. her dogs. They licked her face. Paula gets in her rig. Neither seem to notice her. Seeing her ex-girlfriend was leaving in the rig. She follows until they take the freeway. Heading home. Mad at herself for her cheating. She can't stop putting her down at every chance she can. She wonders why she can't stop. When she knows she has a bad habit of putting her down which she hates. She is home unloading things in her SUV. Wishing her ex-girlfriend would say yes. She was mad at her again. she sees her oldest grandson helping she helps her younger grandson out. He runs inside. He asked his mother. When do we eat. Soon. She has him get in the shower. She washed him. Cleans his hair. I saw Diana today. Really? She rode in grandma's taxi. Oh brother. Knew her mother going to be a bad mood. Get yourself dressed. I need to help your grandma. Okay mother. He was dressing. He goes to watch TV with his brother.

Mother what happen today. Oh, much really. Mother. Okay. My ex-girlfriend needed to go to CVS. It was okay. She picks up medication. She said, I asked her did you pick up pain pills. She said, no I got calcium with vitamin D3. And told me off telling me she doesn't take pain pills. I said, You did before. She was getting madder by the minute. I had a prescriptions for them. Did not buy them off the street. Mother will you please stop bugging her about the pain pills. I could not help putting her down like always. Yet you want her. Yes, dam it. Now she has a new girlfriend. Who wasn't please I was there. Mother. I was the one who was into drugs. Yet you blame her for legal use of her pain medication. She did not make me do it. So, stop bugging her. I can't. It's all I must try to get her back. You will never get her back ever. Then why does she use my taxi. You are losing customers more each day. You should be happy she wanted a ride. Now it will not be even her. you are so stupid mother. She was slapped. You will not bad month your mother. The boys came into the kitchen. They yell you stop hitting mama grandma. The youngest said, I hate you grandma. She was being nice to you. You hurt her feelings. I like the truck her lady friend had. It was nice. Her oldest grandson said. I wish I had seen it too. He giggles they go to their bedroom. He shows him. Wow nice one. Boys dinner. They watch the looks on their mama and grandma. Not talking to each other.

Diane was in the sleeper while Paula finds a safe spot, she has seen another women park. She pulls between two motorhomes. She was in the sleepers noticed Diane was naked grinning. Paula was in the sleeper quickly. Closed the heavy leather curtain. Wait she said, she was back out of the sleeper. She made sure the doors were locked. She closed the curtains on the window. She undressed and was in the sleeper, over her girlfriend. She was kissing her the way she likes doing it. French kissing was more arousing. Diane clearly was willing that was for sure. They were having another wild time in the bed. Diane was looking at her with her hair so messy. I want you to be my full-time girl. Yes, I will Paula. The smile on her face told her a lot. She has wanted her from the beginning like she did.

The rig was there full-full when she wasn't on the road. The dogs loved Paula too. They hear. Let's go girls they wait to be picked up. Diane was always helped in first. Then handed the dogs next. The ex-girlfriend stops coming over. When she came, she was rarely there. When she was her girlfriend was there. They were clearly a couple now. She hated she never would look at her. It was always the one thing that had hope she wanted her back. Her know it all behavior was a total turn off. Every woman she might be interested in were annoyed with her.

She refuses to understand she wasn't so important. She was a taxi driver. Using her taxi to find another woman. But always turns out to be her fault in nearly all the cases of the breakup. The one who got her under her skin and knew how to make her body feel the excitement as she had taken her each time. Was spending all her time with new her girlfriend. It was making her upset she was getting another woman in bed and probably getting her body as well. She had her one time after so many times being taken. The woman found from others the knowledge was reflexed in her characters along with other things she knew was search through so many books. She did not understand her books did sale. She is just a taxi driver without her hack license or the right insurance she must have. She still speeds too much.

She saw her soon on the News talking things she has done. even all the research that leads to her stories. She was making a name for herself. Even her art was being noticed around the world. Her book covers were also noticed. Her ex-girlfriend was making a big difference in her own life. She was even driving the rig. She was shocked how she kept surprising her with so much she can do compared to her. She can't believe she was noticed for other things she wrote. She was feeling small. She is making her feel small for years she thought. Because she was able to get the fire from her temper. All she needed was a woman who could she was not someone who could not think like she did. Telling her she was nothing. Even tried to tell her how publishing was. When she had so many books out. Still working hard doing them. Even spending time on her down time writing and still self-publishing her books. She had done more in her later years than she was doing.

One day she was losing her memory. As she sees her ex-girlfriend still driving her shared Rig with her longtime girl. They were still active in their bed. she has no one. Lost her oldest girl to drugs. Her youngest had a busy life. No time any longer to come to see her in the rest home. She was checking out on the books of one of her mother's ex-girlfriends. She sees she was driving a rig. There was a book of their photo by their rig, with their two dogs. She bought the book. Learns she was also the artist she has art from. Her body tone and she look younger somehow. She was a looker now. She went up to her. She saw she knew her. She was told to come to her. She was feeling like she was on cloud nine. She hugs her. You have turned out so beautiful. My dear. She was by herself. She was missing her love of her life. But she was changed in many ways. After being with a beautiful werewolf. She sees a look of desire in her eyes for her. She has her go into her rig anyway. She was not related but she wanted what she seems to know she could do. Her mother was the past. She takes her for hours. But was incredibly careful with her. She whispers I must leave. I have work to do. She takes the time they had together from her as she had her turn to not see her as she left. The woman returns home feeling so wonderful. Not remembering she has been with one woman she had wanted. But would not act on.

Diane roams the Highways driving her rig. She has new yorkies in her rig. they are playing and their yips keeps her focus as she drives deep into the night. Laying with women and females as she wants them. Diane sees one she must see if she needs help. Pulling over she gets out of rig. Making sure there was man around. She walks to her. She was swearing at the pickup. You had to get a flat in the middle of the forest
I have no way to get you off or buy a replacement she turns to see a hot woman trucker walking up to her.

Told her let's get your pickup, onto my trailer honey. She walks up to her. You by change beautiful a lesbian. I am honey. I will handle her very carefully; she pulls her rig and trailer in front of her pickup. She uses a com-along to pull it up the ramps. She was watching as she was watching her doing it. She saw her use blocks to help keep it attached. Then using a tarp to cover it completely. She has the tie downs tightly holding it down. Then she helps her up in her rig. Diane inhales her womanly scent. She hears a moan from her. You need attention I can tell. Yes, I do. Good. I think a better spot is needed. Yes beautiful. Helping her up on her Rig. she was making sure she has her seat belt on. Kissed her. Gets down. Locks her door. Goes and gets in her driver side. They are back on the freeway. I am Cookie. I am Diane. Nice to meet you, they said, at the same time.

They were going North. Cookie sees a group of men she had seen go by asking if she could handle them. She gave them the finger earlier. Diane. Those are the men who had slowed down and asked if I could handle them all I gave them the finger. Okay honey. I can drive longer. Diane noted the plate number and much more. She made a call to the paranormal highway patrol relaying what she was told. She told them she was going to continue driving awhile longer.

She told the female where she thought they be safer. She said I will be there Diane. Thanks Chief. She growls low. She did not growl back. The Chief seem to understand she was with a human. But she likes Diane. She pulls behind her rig. Saw the pickup was on her trailer. Smart female not leaving a woman helpless on the side of the freeway. The men were all put down. They were planning to put her through hell. If they had found her. What they had in the car meant they have done this several times.

She was heard coming to her rig. She told her to dress she does. Kissed Diane. Diane kissed her harder. Said the Chief of Highway patrol is coming up on her driver side. She was wearing one of Diane's shirts. It fit snuggling. She was kissing her again. When she hears the flashlight knocking on her rig. She takes a mint. Gives Cookie one too. Diane is getting down the Chief was rubbing her ass. She turns as she gets down. She sniffs the Chief. She was telling her get inside this side. Hurry female she whispers in her ear. That has the female rushing inside. She said hi Cookie. Forgive me I need help from Diane. She just grins. May I join you both? They both grin. Sure honey. The rig was moving a lot. Females pulled on both sides. They knew the rig well. They can see she was remarkably busy.

Seeing the highway patrol of the Chief behind her trailer. Said, she must be getting a lot of attention. There was a faith scent of a female in heat. With Diane single she was one they could ask getting attention. They did see a pickup under her tarp. She was not normally carrying a vehicle on her flat bed. it was big items she carried. She clearly had placed it on without using her forklift. When 3 came out than just 2 they were curious of course. All three were marked. The Chief was clearly taken. By Diane and her first being the human and the Chief herself. She had gone to her car. Radio in. I need my car pickup. She told them where she was. She was giggling. No not needing a tow thank you. I am mated to my two mates. She was being teased. Deputy Chief you know who I have been in love with. I am with two.

Yes two. No, I don't think she would, but I am not the one to ask. Okay. Remember I said I have two. Okay. If she says yes, you will need another driver. She was giggling when a man came to her car. She hung up quickly. Diane was there so quickly, and Cookie was as well. Then even more women were rushing up. He was leaving quickly. He has big gut. He did not know she would have anyone looking out for her so fast. He knew she had given him a ticket for having his load way over the allowed length past the trailer without a red flag on the end. It was against the law to have it so far over the flatbed trailer bed. When he sees three in one highway cars. He going to buy the safety flags he must have. The pipes were so far over. A 4-wheeler might end up having it going into their windshield. He was tying it in place. He was ordered to tie them together by The Deputy Chief. He had to go back and buy rope and tape. He was getting even madder. But he needed the job. He has already been warned by his bosses.

He goes to another of the truck stops in the location to keep out of trouble. He was checking out his tires saw he needs air in 4. He does not want to spend all his money on tires. He likes to be with lot lizards a lot. No other woman would bother with him. They liked how he always paid over what their pimp would demand they get. He watched for them. One ran to his rig. she asked can you get me out of here before he comes back Robert. He grins. Sure. He was on the freeway and gone when the pimp looking for his whores. One was missing again. Dam it. he lets her off in Texas. He told her to all of it and get as far as she can go. He had to get his load handled. She calls a friend. pick up and let's head home. Canada. Yes. Hurry. Okay she was there. They went as far up as they could go and found a place to live. And they were dress different than she was always told to dress. To show what she had. He thought maybe she be trying to hitch hike back to Ohio. He would never find her again. she was working good job. Helping to bring in money with her girlfriend. They had finally decided to make it happen at last.

Timer Was Set

Okay let's step behind the boulders. They see an old pickup coming up the hill she did not see anything about a mining company blasting the side of the mountain. It was illegally being done. They had already set the explosive off. She was going by as fast her old pickup could go. She just made it. But the ground was opening a wide crack. She yells come on old girl hurry. It was going faster downhill. She was barely staying ahead of the crack opening. She turns onto a pathed road was gone. She was wiping her brow. That was a close call old girl. She coasted the rest of the way to the local gas station. Made a call before she could gas up old girl.

She asked too strong women if they be so kind to push old girl to the pump. They asked and what would mama like from us after. She was giggling. Hold on you hot things. She was giggling easy girls. May I talk to Chief Tony. Tell her Mama Jo must report an illegal explosion on the pass. I was trying to get old girl to go faster. The area is falling apart quickly. The women were concern that was already dangerous now not safe at all. They go push the old pickup to the pump. One was waiting as the other went in to have her tank filled. Told the folks in the store the pass has become too dangerous for anyone to drive their vehicles through Old Girl barely made it. They saw that Mama Jo was still on the phone. Who is she talking to? Chief Tony. There many came outside just as several police came. She said I know what it sounds like. The ground was cracking as I went through. They thought I could not seem them. You show us Mama Jo. She walks with the rest following her. She was soon trying to watch where she was going. They were doing the same. Now seeing why, she had said, what she is telling her. Everyone please do as you see her do. It's extremely dangerous. The two who have a crush on Mama Jo were staying up with her in case she will need help.

The men were heard. Hurry guys. I see a lot in here. They had blown the area for gems. What they thought was gems was in a place a man was living and he was killed. They found that out quickly. Dam it. we blow an old man up. Here look. They found they had hit the wrong location. They were rushing to the vehicles and leaving. Found they had destroyed the road. One truck has fallen into the crack. They were going the way the law was heading. They were ordered to stop or be shot. They do. Watching the same older woman in the lead. She slabs every man. You killed a good friend of mine. I just brought him food. She was crying. She was carried back with the two who want her as their shared mate. She was wiping her eyes with a shirt one of the strong sexy women. You girls plan to claim me she asked between hic ups. They whisper so she only hears their answers. She looks at the Chief with a certain look. She nods slightly okay I am going on the limb and say yes. The Chief smiles. The men were coming with them. Shaken they had killed an old man. Not knowing there was a cave that close to town.

Mama Jo goes to stay with her two bodybuilders. She was on the bed so quick and waiting naked. They see her waiting for them naked. The females rip their clothes off and on the bed. Looking at her body with lusty looks. It was turning her on quickly. They make her their mate. They were in her motorhome. She was turning not long after she was taken. They always work as a team. The Chief was there after filing the report. She was bringing her purple roses and a super large box of chocolates. She has had a sweet tooth this woman. They have seen each other. Now she can make hers at last. Her werewolf wanted her from the moment she first sniffed her.

Mama Jo was loving all the attention was getting from all of them. She was a werewolf now. She was soon showing them she can take them as well. They were wanting her as their alpha mate. She agreed. She was a great lover to her mates. She still get all the loving she can get. Having the ability was so wonderful.

Watch Out Ladies

The Chief was having a serious meeting with her women of the private police. We have an older Author who has requested our protection. They were sitting up straight. You will rotate your time with her. Why is she asking for protection? She has several trying to get her attention. Younger women with a hero worshiping issues. She isn't into younger. So, you older women have the detail. I am going to be first of course. She has seen a look on the older women faces. She was a favorite author to all of them. She shows her photo to only them. They were werewolves needing a good mate. She was just what they all are hoping for to bed. Having the owner going first was rare. Oh, before I forget. Please get caught up on the easier jobs. I want things corrected. If you need help you reach out to your supervisors.

She was rushing to get done what she needed. She was hoping to seduce that hot woman. She was dressed in her sexiest and revealing dress suit. She goes to get flowers and chocolates. She had made sure she was going to be there. She drives into her driveway. She was bending over grabbing the box of candy and flowers. She was on the passenger side. She hears her moving up to her. You smell good my dear. Oh my god. You are naughty touching me. I figured you wore that hot outfit to let me know you want my touches on your hot body my dear. She was up on her. Slipping her hand up her skirt. She was breathing hard from her boldness. Then she hears her say. Stand up honey. We have unwelcome company. She was up and acting as her bodyguard quickly. One well aimed kick has two men down. Just as a police car was driving slowly through the RV park.

They stopped pick up the two men. Good kick my dear. She smiles and waves as she was making her way up to her. Her client was told to stay in her travel trailer. She locks her car. She was inside. She was watching as she placed the chocolate in the refrigerator. She was bending down as she was. She feels her hands on her ass. She is helped to stand. Helps her turn to face her. She was being kissed by this woman with skills she wants on her right then.

They were soon kissing with a need that shocks both. They were in her bed. They had all the windows, vents and the door. Curtains were shut. She was on top taking her mate again. She looks at the time. Get dress my darling. We must hurry. They are outside. See the older females ready too. She smiles at all of them. The wanting looks told her she was going to be taken by them too.

They were blocking males. The younger females were now doing the blocking with a group of Red Lady Ops. When they joined them. It was getting remarkably interesting. The younger private police were pairing off with the bigger older females. One was selected by 6. She grins. Then growls. They were following her lead. She was encircling one male. He was quickly leaving. Howling to get the rest to leave with him.

The females were still hanging with the Red Lady Ops. They were going to get a safe room and mate them as their mates. They were checking on their boss and the other older females. They finally had a good look at the one they all wanted. They leave notes that were found by their boss. She was giggling our mates younger protection are in safe rooms with their Red Lady Ops. Mates. They were smiling. As they see their hot mate sneaking up on her first mate. She could feel her getting closer.

The female was excited by her trying it. She lets her get as close as she thought she would get. Turns and caught her. Kissed her firmly. She has her moaning now. Carrying her prize back to the bed. She was on her a lot that long night. She looked so hot in her werewolf. When she returns, she was looking so much younger, and she was built even bigger. She was smiling at all 6 mates. No more limp either.

The End